Sweet Sorrow, Bitter Joy

Sweet Sorrow, Bitter Joy

A Novel

Lesley Robinson

iUniverse, Inc.
New York Bloomington Shanghai

Sweet Sorrow, Bitter Joy

Copyright © 2008 by Lesley Robinson

All rights reserved. No part of this book may be used or reproduced by any means, graphic, electronic, or mechanical, including photocopying, recording, taping or by any information storage retrieval system without the written permission of the publisher except in the case of brief quotations embodied in critical articles and reviews.

iUniverse books may be ordered through booksellers or by contacting:

iUniverse
1663 Liberty Drive
Bloomington, IN 47403
www.iuniverse.com
1-800-Authors (1-800-288-4677)

Because of the dynamic nature of the Internet, any Web addresses or links contained in this book may have changed since publication and may no longer be valid.

This is a work of fiction. All of the characters, names, incidents, organizations, and dialogue in this novel are either the products of the author's imagination or are used fictitiously.

ISBN: 978-0-595-45871-4 (pbk)
ISBN: 978-0-595-69748-9 (cloth)
ISBN: 978-0-595-90173-9 (ebk)

Printed in the United States of America

For My Girlie

One

Young men's love then lies
Not truly in their hearts, but in their eyes.
—William Shakespeare *Romeo and Juliet* Act II, Scene 3

Little Stonewick, Hampshire, 1907

I *am* her mother. I have always been her mother. She was my girlie. I have loved her all her life just like any mother would. From the first moment they put her in my arms I knew she was always going to be mine. That day was so full of joy and sadness for me. Yes, joy and sadness at the same time. It's funny like that, life is. It was the very same day that I lost my own sweet baby girl, gone to God. How could that be? She was such a miracle, but then she was taken away from me like a cruel trick. I held both of them that same day, the one in despair and the other in consolation. When I took my own newborn in my arms she was still warm and wet from my body. How could she not be alive? I needed to hold her. I rocked her and cried, keeping her warm and wet with my tears, but then I had to let her go.

Fate was kind to me, though. My husband, God rest his soul, was a gardener, working on a fine estate. It was a Jacobean mansion that had been in the family for centuries. The gardens were a picture and my old man was very proud of his part in keeping everything so beautiful. We lived in a cottage in the village, just next to the estate. I used to do sewing work, alterations and repairs mainly and sometimes I'd get to work on things for the family in the big house. They even had me do things for the nursery when they were expecting at the same time as us. I made some hand embroidered little sheets for the cradle and matching curtains for the windows, much fancier than anything I was planning for my own little one. I didn't need a fancy nursery and an heirloom cradle like they had. I just wanted my baby in my arms—I don't think I was really planning ever to put her down!

Fate was kind to me all right. Their baby turned out to be born that same day and the mistress had a terrible time. Apparently there were doctors and nurses galore, all with their opinions and while I laboured with just my midwife telling me what to do, they all faffed around her like bees around a honey pot from what I heard, boiling water, bringing towels, talking to each other in professional whispers. The labour lasted for a day and a half and apparently her ladyship nearly died. She lost a lot of blood and was very ill. There was no way she was going to be able to feed that baby herself, even if she'd wanted to. I don't know who it was who thought of me, but someone did and it seemed like the perfect solution. I had milk and the baby needed it and I thank God for bringing us together.

When they brought my girlie to me she too was warm, but she was warm with life. She was in a deep sleep, so I unwrapped her and held her against my naked body. It was such a comfort to me. She was warm and she was soft and she smelt of life. It's a wonderful thing that baby smell. There's nothing like it. When you put your cheek against that soft head and you breathe it in. You breathe in all that warmth and the life. Every mother knows that feeling. It's wonderful and it's pure. It's pure love. I hardly gave a thought to the woman whose arms were empty. I needed this baby and I had her. She was mine. Now when I think back, I wonder what *she* was thinking, what *she* was feeling that day. Was she angry? Was she sad that she didn't have her baby to hold? Maybe not. Maybe she was just relieved it was all over and she could just go back to her life. That's what she was expecting, after all. The baby was just a necessary interruption. My plan was something totally different. I was going to be a mother. I was going to have a baby to hold and to love. I needed her more. I remember whispering to her, "Hello, girlie. You're my girlie. I'm the one who loves you. I'm your mama." I counted her fingers and her toes, just like I always knew I would. I don't know why. She was perfect, however many fingers and toes she had, but it was just a way of taking her in, of staking my claim to my baby.

It was a comfort to both of us to put her to my breast and then she was really mine. She rooted and she nuzzled and I pulled her in close to me. She opened that little mouth like a great big yawn, like a baby bird, waiting for a worm. How did she know what to do? I suppose it's all just part of the same miracle of life. It was a miracle that she was healing my aching heart. I needed to give her my milk, to give her my mothering, to give her my love. After all, what is being a mother all about? It's about getting to know your baby and being there all the time. You hold her all day long and you sleep cuddled up next to her at night and you're there whenever she needs you. You breathe together and you both need each other. You wake up a moment before she stirs and you wonder how nature could have arranged things so perfectly. It's about following your instincts and following your heart. That's all there is to it really. And the woman who gave birth to her didn't know anything about it. That really is something to pity.

Well, what can I say about what has happened? It wasn't supposed to end like this, that's for sure. "Love makes life worth living," was what my girlie said to me. Yes, she really did say that. I thought at the time what did she know? What did she know about life and love? About the real love that life is all about? The kind that lasts forever, whatever happens. She always was so strong-willed and independent. My old man, God rest his soul, always used to say so. Oh no, it was never supposed to end like this. I should have known it was going to end in disaster, I should have protected her from all the bad stuff. But just as things can go from seventh heaven to the depths of despair in the blink of an eye, what is a calamity today can turn into a delight tomorrow. That's how life is and you have to make the best of what you've got. She didn't know that. How could she? I should have kept her safe from all the hurt. That was my job.

So many memories! She was a beautiful baby and I was the one who knew everything about her. The day that she and my poor little one were born, I was born as a mother. I felt like I had somehow partaken of the secret of life. I don't understand how a woman can ever get over giving her child to another woman to nurse, but I thank the Lord that she was given to me; she was the greatest gift anyone could ever hope to receive. What a blessing! She saved me. Does that sound too dramatic? But it's true, she really did save my life, or at least she saved my sanity. But what about the mistress? If I was saved, then how on earth did she manage to carry on without her own flesh and blood to hold and love? I just can't understand it. How do some women fight their instincts? We must all have the same instincts, but some of us can put them first. We can gain confidence from our experience of being mothers. I suppose that was why it was different for her. She never really got to have any of that experience. She never put that baby to her breast. She never formed that unbreakable bond. I pity her. Oh, how I pity her.

We moved into the big house, so that I could be with my girlie night and day. I carried her constantly for those first few months of her life. I used to "wear" my baby. I tied her around me in a sling to keep her close. I just couldn't have managed without that simple strip of fabric. That way I could get on with whatever I had to get on with and the baby was just a part of my life, snuggling into my body, sleeping against me, sharing my warmth. We needed each other. When she needed feeding I was there, when she needed warmth I was there and when she needed comfort I was there. And I needed her too. I needed to know she was close to my body and she was safe. I needed to feed her when I was overflowing with milk and love. It was so simple. Supply and demand. Give and take. There's nothing like that closeness and I'll treasure that memory to my dying day. Yes, I do pity the mistress that she never had that and now she's left with nothing. She has nothing and she knows I have everything that was hers. That *should* have been hers. That *could* have been hers if she hadn't let it go.

Closeness. That's what it was. And the closeness my girlie and I had just grew and grew, just as she was growing every day: growing strong from what she got, only from me. I did it all. I was growing a whole person only on what was coming out of my own body. What magic. It's one of the ordinary miracles of life. Just an ordinary miracle. Her first smile was in answer to my smile. That's amazing, a baby's smile. It's like the biggest thing that ever happened to you, the first time you see it. I suppose it's just another ordinary miracle. Ordinary because it happens all the time, but miraculous because the first time only ever happens once.

Her first taste of real food was a crust she grabbed off my plate. It was so funny. I wasn't paying attention, but my old man, God rest his soul, just pointed at her from across the table, laughing silently. I looked down at her in my lap and she grinned up at me, a toothless grin with her face covered in crumbs. I could have eaten her up on the spot! You know, I never quite believed that she was really going to start eating just like that, all by herself, when she was ready. People told me that was how it would be, but I never quite believed it till it happened. I suppose it's like so many things with children. They do it when they're ready. You can't make them ready by pushing them. If anything, that has the opposite effect. When you push a child who's not ready that'll just make her clingy. And when they're ready, there's no stopping them.

Her first real word, or what I think of as her first real word, was actually a sign. She must have been about nine months old. One day I offered her a cup of water when she was eating a piece of fruit and she shook her head that she didn't want water. I picked her up and put her to the breast and that was what she wanted. After that she would often shake her head at me when she wanted to nurse. And I reinforced it. I did it back to her. I shook my head at her and I would put her to my breast. It was her sign, her "word" for nursing and it was our own secret language. It was funny and I'd be the only one who knew what she wanted. Sometimes when she wanted to nurse, she would grizzle and pull on my skirt, shaking her head. I'd say to her, "What's the matter my girlie? Are you tired?" and she'd shake her head. And then I'd say, "Are you hungry?" and she'd shake her head. And I would shrug my shoulders and say, "I don't know what she wants." But I *did* know and no one else did. Ah, those were the days,

She began to talk well enough as well though. She was my little chatterbox, talking in complete sentences well before she was two. Such a cutie-pie! We laughed at everything she said. I remember she learnt to say "blue" when she was just eighteen months old and everyone thought she was so clever.

We'd say to her, "Now what colour is this, girlie?" and she would answer, "Blue!" Everyone was amazed that she could know her colours at eighteen months, but we never asked her anything that wasn't blue!

I held her hand as she took her first step and then I let go and watched her walking away from me, out towards the big wide world. Well, she was ready, wasn't she? As I said, they do things when they're ready. You can't make them eat, you can't make them sleep, you can't make them walk. Everything comes in its own sweet time. Oh, it all seems like yesterday, but so much has happened since then. She grew up in an instant. I suppose that when they hit adolescence and they think they know it all, it's like toddlerhood all over again! They're ready to explore, to go out and learn about the world, but they still need you there in the background, just in case they need somewhere safe to come back to.

She had the biggest eyes I've ever seen on a toddler: those soulful, pleading eyes that you could never refuse anything. They were huge and the bluest blue I've ever seen. Maybe it was the fact that she was mine that made her the most beautiful child in all of God's creation. Is it like that for all mothers? I suppose it must be, but she really was beautiful, everybody said it and I was so proud, as if I'd made her myself. I may be no Mona Lisa, but I know beauty when I see it. I suppose in a way I did help to make her who she was by raising her with love and showing her the way to care for people and do the right thing.

They learn by example, don't they? I suppose that's why the sins of the fathers are visited on the children. (Not the sins of the mothers, mind you.)

It near broke my heart to wean her when she turned three. It just didn't feel right to me somehow, but even though I was the one who felt all the motherly things and was teaching her the lessons of trust and love, I was told that there were some things that weren't my decision to make. That hurt me so much. If *I* wasn't her mother, then who was? Tell me that. I put that foul tasting stuff on my nipples like you're supposed to do and she looked at me like I had taken away everything she cared about. I had to give her so much other mothering after that, but I wonder if she ever really forgave me. I was always her island of comfort to come back to when she needed soothing. It was like she was on an invisible cord that would stretch so far and then she'd have to come back for re-fuelling, for reassurance, for a top up of love. That's how babies learn independence and she certainly did that! My old man, God rest his soul, used to laugh at her funny little ways and she used to smile back at him and run off laughing. I'll never forget what happened just the day before she was weaned. She was running about and she fell flat on her face and cracked her head open. My old man, God rest his soul, picked her up and dusted her off.

"Poppet," he said, "if you were a bit more grown up you'd be flat on your back for some lad, instead of flat on your face!" She just smiled so earnestly and said yes. We laughed and laughed. She was a treasure to him too. He called her his poppet. Every child needs a father as well as a mother and he was her father just as I was always her mother. He was there in the background, encouraging and helping her learn about the world. The master and the mistress were so far away from her childhood, even though they were in the same house. I suppose they were too busy being lady and gentleman and doing whatever those upper crust bods do with themselves. I suppose it would have been like that anyway, even if they hadn't needed a wet nurse from day one. They would still have given her over to a nanny. I thank the Lord that circumstances made me the wet nurse and the nanny all in one. It's no wonder I knew that my old man and I were her real parents. We couldn't teach her the book stuff, but we taught her what matters. It was from us that she learnt to love and to live and to laugh. Learning how to love should be the first lesson for every child and I think she was very lucky in that. It's the lesson a baby learns at her mother's breast and I was so lucky to be able to give her that. It's the greatest privilege of my life.

Even after she weaned she still needed me round the clock. I was at least glad that the master and the mistress recognised that she needed me and didn't turn us out of the house once she was weaned and I didn't seem so useful to them any more. I know they thought that it was just a job for me, but that's not how we saw it, me and my old man. Every night before she went to sleep she used to ask me to give her a hundred kisses. No matter how hard I tried to count to over a hundred, she always said I had missed some and she wanted me to start over. She always needed more. She never seemed to get enough of my stories either. She always wanted me to tell her stories about when I was a little girl, about things my mother said and did and she loved the stories of my big brother who was always such a stinker to me, but I loved him all the more for it. He was my best friend growing up and I suppose that was something that my girlie never had. She could never get enough of those stories anyway. As soon as I was finished she would be begging me to tell it all over again.

And she loved it when I would lean over to her and whisper, "Do you want to know a secret, girlie?"

She would look up at me from under those thick eyelashes of hers and whisper back, "Yes." Then I would pause dramatically and look around to make sure no one would hear the secret.

"I love you," I would whisper.

Then she would laugh and say out loud, "I knew that."

Then I would say, "And how do you know that?"

"You told me a thousand times."

Or sometimes she would say, "I'm a daughter. A daughter knows these things."

That was because I would often say, "I'm a mother. A mother knows these things," when I couldn't explain something I just knew by instinct.

She still needed me in the middle of the night too. I rocked her in my arms as she told me about her nightmares. I'll never forget one night, just before dawn when she woke up screaming. She dreamt that there was a volcano behind the house and when it erupted she woke up and found that she had wet the bed. We laughed about that too over the years. I was glad to be there for her at night. No one should have to sleep alone. I remember one morning when I got up early and left her alone in the bed. I think she must have been about four years old. What a kafuffle there was when she woke up. She must have turned herself around somehow while she was sleeping and she woke up with her head down at the tucked-in end of the bed. She set up such a wailing.

"Help, save me," she was shouting, over and over again. When we rushed in and found her, she was thrashing around and screaming with her head right down at the foot of the bed. Afterwards she said she woke up and thought she was dead. No, no one should have to sleep alone.

As she got older she had to learn how to become a lady. I wonder if she was really quite ready for that. She was still just a little girl in so many ways. Yes, she was still a little girl, just my girlie. Perhaps I'm just saying that now because I couldn't bear thinking that I would lose her. I would lose my child and *I* wasn't ready for that. I always knew that she had to grow up and grow away from me. Well, I suppose I was proud that I was raising a lady. She was becoming so beautiful and independent. Of course I was proud I was raising a lady and such a fine one too. She used to complain that she had to go and learn all those ladylike accomplishments. She had to go to singing lessons and learn to play the piano and speak some foreign lingo. She hated going to take these lessons and she'd whine and say it was too hard and she just wanted to stay with me. I'd say she was being a silly billy because wherever she went, even if I couldn't go with her, my love was always with her. This always made her giggle because she thought that was so silly. It didn't matter to me that she thought it was silly. It made her laugh and that was good enough for me. And *I* knew that it was true. When a child grows up, she may go away from you, but she can't go without your love. It keeps her safe. It keeps her topped up. Even when your children are really off on their own, your love is still with them whether they like it or not. They can never leave it behind. That's how it is with mother's love.

And then there was *him*. I always knew that boy was going to be trouble. It wasn't just that he came from that family. There was lots of talk about him, so dashing and good looking. He seemed to be pretty popular with the ladies. He had a dark and moody look about him which made him mysterious and attractive, I suppose. With his soft skin and patchy bumfluff I saw him as just a boy, but he obviously thought of himself as a ladies' man. Why, it was only a few weeks before that he was madly in love with some other girl and mooning around because she wouldn't give him the time of day. Everybody knew it. He was just a six foot bundle of hormones and trouble: always fighting and wooing. There was no half way with him. He was always quick to passion: whether it was in love or in anger. I sigh just at the thought of it. It was almost as if he enjoyed getting into scrapes and the family troubles were just an excuse for him: always hanging around with that band of high-strung, no good troublemakers. The families had been at each other hammer and tongs for as long as anyone could remember. Even the below stairs lot would fight each other in the market place over at Great Stonewick, yelling insults at each other, saying each master was better than the other, as if anyone really cared. They were just trying to score points off each other. What a load of silly old nonsense! Who knows what even started all the animosity between the two families, but it had been going on for donkeys' years and there he was, that boy, right in the thick of it, trading insults, goading the others, leaping on any opportunity to get into a fight. I couldn't for the life of me see what she saw in him. I suppose it was the excitement, the adventure of it and the thrill of what is forbidden. That seems to go a long way in making something seem like something more than what it really is.

Maybe they thought they could bring their families together with their love and end the stupid feud. That was all very well, but they didn't even think about going about things in anything like a "proper" way. What were they thinking? There was no asking for her hand, no meeting to ask her father's permission, no handshake. Well, how could there be? There couldn't *be* any sort of meeting with the likes of him. There were no introductions, no get-together of the families. It just wasn't proper at all, but maybe that was why they hoped it would work out. They were trying to forge their own path in the midst of all that rottenness. Once they were married no one could object to the union, could they? They'd all have to forever hold their peace. There was of course the added complication that the master had actually already shaken hands with someone else. What were they thinking? I suppose they weren't thinking at all, were they? They were just caught up in the moment and letting it happen, like a pebble rolling down a hill, going faster and faster. Even though it's just a pebble, there's no stopping it. It's got too much energy, a life all of its own. I suppose young love is like that. There's no stopping it and there's certainly no logic. You can't speak up against it because you can bet your life no one will be listening.

And my part in all this misery? I helped get her into this God-awful mess. I only did what I did out of love for her. Of course I knew it was always bound to end in tears, but sometimes the tears are worth it. I'd be there to help dry her eyes and she'd learn a good lesson about what's really important in life. That was what I thought and I don't think I was wrong, even now. And I wasn't the only one. There was that vicar chappy. You'd think he'd mean well, wouldn't you and he *was* a clergyman, after all. You'd think he would know all about doing the right thing, wouldn't you? He just wanted to put an end to all this stupid feuding and he thought that this would be a way to do it. I suppose I can't blame him for that. I certainly never imagined it would go this far. I wanted her to love and learn, but not like this. I wanted it to be a happy learning. I thought she would just get it out of her system and then get on with the real stuff of marriage and family. No one expects that there will be only one love in their life. No one except my girlie. Look at me! I had a few little adventures of my own in my time. I'm afraid I wasn't pure as the driven snow when I met my old man, God rest his soul. Far from it, but that was what made me know it was time to settle for just one man, the right one. He didn't have to be dashing and romantic. It was like putting on a baggy old jumper when I met him. He was comfortable and just right for me. A good fit. Once I met him I didn't need all that other stuff any more. What luck I had to meet the right man and to keep him.

"Love makes life worth living." Yes and you live one day at a time, never knowing what the next will bring.

Stonewick Park, Hampshire, 1907

I'm her mother. I wish I could be honoured to say so, but the honour would be a dubious one. I remember the pain of her birth. I feared it and when it came I just wanted it to be over. I was told that it was a "good" pain, but that didn't help me to conquer it. I yelled and shrieked my way through it, blaming my husband and the doctors and even blaming God, for all the good it did me. And when it was over there was nothing left. I felt a tremendous relief that the pain was over, that I had survived and the baby was a healthy one. Beyond that I felt a total numbness, a great void that I didn't know how to fill. I'm not sure what I was supposed to feel, but that's what I remember: an overwhelming nothingness.

When I was a girl I always knew that this was going to be my destiny. I expected to make a good marriage and to produce healthy heirs to carry on the family name. I did what was expected of me, yet somehow I was cheated. I did my duty. I haemorrhaged after the delivery and was so ill, I couldn't feed the baby myself and I gave my child over to the wet nurse, so that my body could recover and the baby would thrive. If I could recover quickly from the rigours of childbirth and I could try again to produce a male heir. But I was cheated. I did all that I was supposed to do and the son and heir was never born. The girl was all there was and I had handed her over. I was left to make the best of it, feeling forever guilty in my own heart that what had happened was somehow my fault.

I always felt like an observer of her childhood. I watched her grow, although I felt as though I were somewhat of a bystander in her life. It was like watching a play from the third row of the audience. There were times when I knew I could have written the script better and I was able to voice my opinions as a critic might. I could influence the next act. After all, I was the mistress and although for me there was always a feeling of emptiness and ineptitude for the task of motherhood, I still held power in the relationship. It was up to me to decide which accomplishments my daughter would learn and when. She was to become my successor, a mirror image of myself and I was responsible for her preparation for her future role as lady, as wife and as mother.

It seemed to me that from the early days my daughter had a rebellious streak in her and that silly nurse only reinforced it with her indulgence. To her the girl could do no wrong and she allowed her affection for her to get in the way of teaching her discipline. When I insisted upon it I was made to feel the villain. I knew however, that she needed to be adequately prepared for what was to come and it was my duty to insist upon it. My husband too treated her with indulgence. She was his precious jewel and she was able to twist him around her little finger with her beauty and her charm. Even when she was just a small girl, his only desire was to spoil her rotten. And look where all this indulgence has led. The girl threw away her whole life on a wilful whim. At least I did what I could and I can be satisfied in the knowledge that it was not I who was at fault. I can absolve myself of the responsibility; but I am still left with that same emptiness that I have experienced from the day she was born and that same guilt that has *gnawed away at me that all the family's fortunes were invested in this one wayward child. I knew intellectually that I was not responsible, but still I felt guilty somewhere in my gut.*

I cannot allow myself to give in to self doubt. The girl showed no respect for the family name and no respect for those of us who had indulged her and given her so much. She owed that respect in return. She was our pride and joy and we are left to mourn because of her callous disregard for all that we hold dear. She did it in the name of love. How naively selfish of her to have imagined that her young "love" could supersede the dignity and the enduring esteem of the family name. It is the selfishness of the young. We all have to make sacrifices in life and she would have found them to be worthwhile in the long run. Every girl would wish to marry for love, but can anyone expect that sort of love to last? Duty and nobility are enduring when the first flower of passion has withered and died. I too might have been tempted to defy my father, but I had the wit to defer to his wisdom in such matters and I have led a good and respectable life.

And the boy ... I can't even bring myself to mention his name. What promises he must have made to her. Why would she even hear him, knowing who he was and where he came from? (Perhaps only in defiance of her parents.) Had she only shared her feelings with me, I would at least have had the opportunity to show her the folly of trusting such a man. I say man, but he didn't merit the label. He was never more than a duplicitous coward, interested only in the pleasure of the moment, at the expense of all of those around him, even those he purported to love and respect. He didn't even merit his own abhorrent name.

There are other people I blame as well, perhaps even more than him. The vicar certainly should have known better. And the nurse ... well I suppose you couldn't expect anything else from her. If I ever see her again it will be too soon. Why did she know my daughter's secret thoughts when I was cut out so cruelly? They would giggle together like schoolgirls while I yearned to be party to her girlish hopes and dreams. I could only look on and smile as though I didn't care, as though it was a natural thing for them to be so complicit and for me to be so left out. I had to appear indulgent and benevolent, whatever pain I was feeling. I had to keep my distance. What on earth were the vicar and the nurse thinking? They were supposed to be the responsible adults. As hard as I try to think of their best possible motives, I just can't imagine how they could have thought they were doing the right thing. I do *want to think the best of them. Really I do, but how could encouraging her to defy her parents be the right thing? How could letting her ruin her life be the right thing? I can't imagine and I can't forgive them. They took my daughter away from me just as much as he did.*

Two

All the trouble began when she was still really just a slip of a girl. I suppose she wasn't such a bad age to be thinking about love and marriage. I knew her age to the day because of my own poor little lamb. I knew it better than my mistress. You see, I *am* her mother. It was a fortnight before her birthday. I'll never forget that day. It's there, etched into my memory, written in indelible ink, so to speak. I was alone in my girlie's room, folding countless articles of discarded clothing that she had tried on in front of the mirror and thrown down on the floor. Her ladyship came flouncing into my girlie's room all in a tizzy, saying she wanted to speak to her. She was all secretive with her sideways looks and her little smiles. I wondered what all the fuss was about and since I was as curious as a kitten with a ball of yarn in a basket, I called my girlie for her. I went to the top of the stairs and called her. I went along the corridor and called her. I called and I called and I knew she wasn't far away, but would she come when I called her? It's like I said, she was all independence and doing her own thing. Finally she came, breezing in without a care in the world. No matter that I had just about yelled myself hoarse trying to get her to come.

Her ladyship went all mysterious, saying I should leave so they could talk in private. That just got me all the more curious. How disappointing though, to get me all excited and expectant and then to send me away! That was what she was like though; always blowing hot and cold and you never quite knew where you stood with her. Next thing I knew she'd changed her mind and wanted me to stay. Well I never! I expect she thought I'd have influence over my girlie in important things. I wonder if her being like that was something to do with her bitterness over never having another child. Isn't that why the posh people use wet nurses? So they can get their body right back into production, so to speak? As far as her body was concerned, it was *her* baby who had died, not mine. I can't imagine anything that would have made *me* more bitter. She was bitter alright and although she never said anything, I would catch her looking at me with what I thought must have been envy. She gave me her baby, hoping to give her husband a son and then it never happened. I had my girlie to love. She had nothing. Well, nothing except power and wealth I suppose. Maybe that was why it was so important to her to treat me like the servant that I was. My position in the household was a special one. I was just a servant, so I had to remember my place, but I was a special kind of servant. I wasn't one of the below stairs lot. In a way I was one of the family. My job was more important than any other servant's. All the same, she had power over me because I was doing her job—being mother to her child. You'd think there was no one else in the world who could be mother to your child. Not if you were a real mother, doing the mothering, not just giving birth. Anyway, it did give her power over me. What if she took up against me and sent me away? What would have become of my girlie? It's a terrible thing for a mother to lose a child. How would it be for a child to lose her mother?

Where was I? Oh yes, she started talking about how old my girlie was and I told her right there and then I knew her age to the day because of my poor little lamb. She got me into a right load of reminiscences, oh my! Three years after she was born was when she was weaned. Yes, it was just about three years to the day. It reminded me of what a cute little three year-old she was and I found myself telling her ladyship that story of how she fell over and cracked her head open and my husband, God rest his soul, made that joke about being flat on her back. And how we laughed over that! It's funny how things come back to you. Yes, here I go again. The mistress didn't seem to be in the mood to listen to my stories, but I just doubled up laughing until she told me in no uncertain terms to quit my nonsense. She was just jealous. Bitter and jealous. Jealous cow.

The next thing I knew, she was asking my girlie what she thought about getting married. Now as far as I was concerned seeing her married was something I had thought a lot about. After all, wasn't that what I was raising her for, to become a lady and make a fine marriage? How exciting that the master and the mistress thought it was time and her such a beauty and all. Yes, she was getting to that age, when the urges are starting to stir. I suppose it was time for her to be thinking about love and that, although one day I'd look at her and see the beautiful young woman she was becoming and the next, she'd still seem to be a little girl. It was as though she was my little girl in what was becoming a woman's body, still with her big blue eyes and her blond curls, but with a woman's shape. My girlie, growing up. Instead of being a little doll, she was becoming an exquisite lady and any gentleman would be lucky to have her.

Her ladyship said, "Well, young lady, it's high time for you to be thinking about marriage, you know. There are plenty of girls younger than you who are married and mothers too." (That was true enough.) "Why," she went on, "I was only your age when you were born. It certainly is time for you to be thinking about marriage." It was hard to believe that the mistress was really that young. That made her a lot younger than me and I can't say she seemed it. It was the bitterness, I suppose. She had that sour, jowly look about her, like she was going to sag into some pretty unattractive wrinkles way before her time. Well, not only had the master and the mistress been thinking about marrying off my girlie, but they had someone all lined up: a fine figure of man and I told her as much. (He wasn't one that *I'd* be kicking out of bed, I can tell you.) Oh my, how exciting. I could hardly wait. Just think, my girlie, a bride so soon. Ooh she'd make a beautiful bride, all dressed up in the white dress with satin and lace and surrounded by flowers. I could just picture it. *I* was so excited I could hardly keep from jumping up and down. I looked over at my girlie and I could see that she wasn't quite as tickled as I was. She had that little frown on her face that I remembered from when she was little, with her nose all wrinkled up. (It was so cute.)

"So what do you think, girl?" said my mistress. (She used to say that: "girl", like she was looking down on her—so different from "my girlie"—that was a loving thing to call her.)

"Do you think you could love him?" she went on. "He has made a special point of asking for you. He met with your father and asked for your hand. It was so formal, but so touching." Well, she went on and on about how handsome he was and how fine and how the only thing he lacked was a beautiful wife on his arm. Well, you couldn't argue with that now, could you? My girlie would certainly be a fine adornment for such a man. I could just picture them together in their finery on their wedding day. Ooh, what a joy that would be. Her ladyship said that we'd have the chance to see for ourselves that very night. He was going to be the special guest at the ball that was being held that evening at Stonewick Park, so she could meet him. I just about squealed with excitement, but my girlie was silent as a doorpost.

"Well fancy that," I said. "I bet having him for a husband would make you the finest lady around." Her ladyship just ignored me. Well, there was nothing new about that. I don't think she gave me credit for a single thought. It was just plain jealousy if you ask me. I had the one thing she didn't. I had the most precious thing and she could only guess how it felt. I had my girlie's love.

She asked her again what she thought about the prospect. I wonder if it mattered really what she thought. They were probably going to make her marry him anyway. I expected that it had already been agreed. I found out afterwards mind you, that the master was not in such a hurry to marry her off at that point after all. He thought she was still a little too young. Nevertheless he encouraged the young man to try to win her affections. After all, it was a very fine match and he certainly didn't want to say no to him. My girlie was his great prize to give away. With no son, the future of the family was all going to be in her hands and a good match was so important to the master. It was a way for him to weigh his status. How much was she worth? That was how the world would judge how much *he* was worth. Disgusting. As if people had a monetary value.

The mistress and I both looked at my girlie expectantly. She didn't seem to be too excited at the prospect, in fact I'd say she was pretty guarded. I don't think she had thought about marriage very much. It was something she saw as being way off in the future—when she grew up. She was too busy being a little girl still, just my girlie.

"Well," said she finally, "I think that I might be able to love him. I would want to because that would make you happy. So if wanting it to happen would make it happen, then I could love him." Well, that would have made me happy too. What a lovely girl, just wanting to please them, to make them happy. Praise the Lord! After all, there's nothing better than a wedding and all its happy excitement and at least she was prepared to think about it. And if she didn't really have a choice I would hope that she *could* love him and know the blessing of a good life with a good man. I could hardly believe it, my girlie about to become a grown up, married lady and what a beautiful bride she would make with her handsome husband by her side (and a rich as well as a handsome one). Ooh!

After her ladyship was gone I could hardly contain myself. I was as excited and giggly as a young girl myself. My girlie wasn't nearly as excited as I was. She seemed quiet and thoughtful, as if she didn't really know what to make of the whole thing. She seemed, well, a little bewildered I'd say.

"Well, girlie?" I said expectantly. I raised my eyebrows at her and waited on tenterhooks.

"Well ...?" I repeated and I leaned forward, raising my eyebrows even higher, like I could get them to go any further!

"Well what?" she replied a little sullenly and with all the innocence in the world.

"What do you mean 'well what'?" I gave her that look again and broke into a giggle.

"Well, it's all new to me all this, isn't it? I don't really know what to think. I suppose I'll get used to the idea, but I really didn't think they would be thinking about this so soon." Well, she was right there.

"I suppose it kind of took you by surprise," I said taking her hand. She nodded and looked down, all modesty and coyness. What a lovely girl!

"Maybe I'm just not ready for this yet," she reasoned, all pensive and demure.

"Well you could do a lot worse," I said. "Believe me you could do a lot worse. Come on, let's go and get you ready to meet the man of your dreams." And I patted her gently on the shoulder, giving her an encouraging little smile. She answered my smile with a loving look. What a lovely girl indeed.

Little did I know that it was someone else altogether that she was going to fall A over T for that night. There's no accounting for a person's feelings. It would all have been so simple if she had taken a fancy to the right one. There would have been none of this misery and everyone would have been happy, her most of all. But there you go. Such is life and love and after all, love makes life worth living!

My husband was not planning to part with our daughter just yet. He had hoped to allow her a couple more years to mature before thinking about a husband for her. On reflection, how right he was that she lacked the maturity to enter into a marriage at her tender age. My husband is a wise man who knows much about the ways of the world. His concern was all for her welfare. He told me that a highly eligible young man was asking for her. What young man would not have been interested in her in the first flower of her growing beauty? I prided myself that in looks at least she was like myself. The nurse had a face like a half-chewed toffee and she always acted like she was responsible for the girl's beauty and grace!

The young man in question was from a good family with plenty of money and influence. This was the kind of match we were seeking for her. She would never want for anything, but would be secure in her life. The joining of the two families would be beneficial to both, increasing the wealth and influence of both and my daughter would forever enjoy the lifestyle to which she was accustomed, perhaps even better than that to which she was accustomed. We only wanted the best for her and this was what we had been preparing for her whole life. My husband, although having wished to wait for a while, did not want to reject this handsome offer. He encouraged the young man, (although he needed little encouragement) to seek to win her affection. And so it fell to me to speak to her and to plant the seed of the idea of marriage to our chosen man in her mind. I'm sure that she too had thought that she had a couple more years of girlhood ahead of her and seemed totally surprised by the suggestion. I had planned to talk to her in private, but I think that the nurse's presence and her open and vociferous pleasure at the prospect of my daughter's marriage was in fact a help in encouraging her acquiescence in the matter. I would have preferred that that woman not be involved in matters of such consequence in my daughter's life. She was so flighty and irritating. It was clear to me then that the woman's advice was not required. A woman of no education, what would she know of such matters? So her counsel was not required. It was her enthusiasm that would be useful to me.

I must say the girl reacted initially with surprise and more than a little bemusement. It appeared that such matters had been the last thing on her mind. Nevertheless, I only sought to plant the seed and to encourage her to receive the man courteously with a view to considering him as her future husband. She agreed to contemplate the prospect and this was all that was required of her for the time being. She certainly seemed completely compliant and no doubt sought to please her father and me. She knew her duty and accepted it obediently. The festivities of that evening presented the ideal opportunity for her to begin to contemplate the prospect of her adult life and the path we had chosen for her. Meeting him that evening would be the occasion for her to consider her future. How could she not be overjoyed at the notion of her life married to such a fine and well-mannered man? I expected gratitude from her for the care we had put into this decision for her and for the advantage which lay ahead of her.

The nurse was fussing and clucking around her like a mother hen. Well, if everything went to plan, we were not going to have to put up with the woman much longer.

Three

What a night it turned out to be!

I don't know how that boy found out about it, but there he was, bold as brass. It seems that his cronies were all wanting to show up uninvited to the ball, just for the hell of it. It turned out that they told him that that other girl he was swooning over was going to be there and that was how they persuaded him to join them. He just wanted to be near her. I don't know! It just shows you he wasn't serious about loving anyone in particular. He just wanted to be in love—he was in love with being in love. What did he think it meant? Poetry and flowers? Or was it just sex? Where are the boundaries? Is it the union of two souls or just two bodies? That's what men are like. They've got to go and spread their seed far and wide. A woman needs just the one man to make her a real woman, to make her a mother and that's the fulfillment of womanhood as far as I am concerned. It's certainly what sex is for (not that it's not fun doing it). But men …

What a marvellous feast it was that night. The master wanted to make a good impression, that was for sure. And what a show he put on! No expense was spared. That was certainly the fanciest spread I'd ever seen laid on. He must have brought in chefs and kitchen staff galore just for the one night. And the champagne was flowing like water. He had spared no expense and he wanted to make sure no one was in any doubt about that. We all stuffed ourselves out in the kitchen. Well, *I* did anyway and I'm not ashamed of that, it was all so scrumptious and you might as well take advantage when something's being offered to you on a plate and that's true literally as well as in a manner of speaking, if you see what I mean.

It was right when the food was being cleared away and the orchestra was getting ready to play that that boy showed up with his cronies. There was all sorts of commotion, what with everything being set up for the dancing. It was pretty easy for them to slip into a ball without causing even a whisper. There were people all over the place: in the ballroom, in the drawing rooms, in the dining room, in the hallways, everywhere, so who would notice a few uninvited guests? The master was pleased enough to have so many guests to show off to. He welcomed one and all and told them to have a jolly good time dancing till they dropped. I think he must have known who they were, but he wasn't going to let a few uninvited rascals spoil his night. I hung around in the corridor between the ballroom and the kitchen and watched that boy mooning around at the edge of the room while the others were dancing up a storm. And then he spotted her. My girlie. He stopped still and just stared at her. What a sight she was that night. A real picture. She was all dressed in blue to show off her eyes. It was a beautiful blue silk gown and her hair was done up in a very grown up way, with just a little wisp of blond escaping playfully over her eyes. I can understand how any young man would fall in love with her right there and then, like a thunderbolt. It was almost as if you heard the thud of the arrow through his heart. Mind you, my old man, God rest his soul, used to say that it wasn't the hearts of young men that stirred when they saw a beauty like that. It was altogether in a different place that his feelings would be roused.

I wasn't fooled by his skulking around and I wasn't the only one who was watching. My girlie's cousin came right over and challenged him. He recognized him straight away as one of "them" and strutted over to pick a fight with him quicker than you could say boo. He went right up to the master and pointed him out. He told his uncle who he was. He told him right out that the boy came from that family and he had come to the ball to have a good laugh at our expense. But the master was very gracious. He wanted to show what a generous host he was, even to uninvited guests. He didn't want any fuss. Well, he wouldn't, would he? He told his nephew that this wasn't the time and the place to be making such a ruckus. Well, it wouldn't look good, would it? The poor lad was quite put out. He said that he didn't want to put up with this sort of behaviour from one of "them", but the master put him in his place quickly enough. He shut him up like a book and the lad turned tail and left with his pride all in tatters, muttering threats to the intruder under his breath. That was what the master was like: always wanting to give the right impression. It was important to him to do the right thing and to make sure everyone noticed. This was his night and no one, neither that boy, nor his own nephew was going to take away his thunder. The nephew didn't take this well to say the least. It was humiliating for him to be put in his place by his uncle over that no good, jumped up little gatecrasher. I wouldn't be surprised if it wasn't right there and then that he vowed to himself to get his own back on him and the sooner the better.

Once that unpleasant little scene was over, that boy, impudent young scallywag that he was, turned his attentions to my girlie and oh, how he charmed her. Before she even had a moment to think, he had grabbed her hand and held on to it ardently. I watched as their eyes met and the fireworks went off. Oh my, I thought, she'll be up till dawn talking about this moment. The look on her face was one I had seen so many times before, but to see it on that fresh and lovely face that I knew so intimately, turned her almost instantly into a stranger to me. In that instant she had become his. Did that mean she was no longer mine? No longer my girlie? Now, suddenly they shared something that I could never be a part of. She was lost, but I rejoiced for her. This was what was supposed to happen tonight—well in a manner of speaking. It was the chosen moment for her to grow up and fall in love. I suppose I'd have to say that I believe in love at first sight—because this was it. I could almost feel the flutter of her heart, the butterflies in her stomach. Oh, the joy of that pure feeling, before it is tainted by knowledge and experience.

They held each other's eyes, whispering coyly and then they kissed for a fleeting moment and then again. Ooh, my heart was going thump, thump, thump as I watched them from the doorway. It seemed to me that it was time for me to intervene before things got out of hand. I coughed and stepped forward.

"Come along, young lady," I said. "Your mother would like a word with you." She stepped back from him obediently, dropping her gaze and flushed, glancing stealthily at him through her eyelashes. I got in between them and started ushering her away from him. It was like pulling a pin off a magnet.

"And who *is* her mother?" that impudent boy asked me, his eyes still searching to make contact with hers again. It was then that I realised that he didn't even know who she was.

"She's the lady of the house," I told him. "So you'd better keep your hands to yourself."

"Oh," he muttered, with his puppy dog eyes and his pouting lip. "She's one of them—that makes us loving enemies—or hateful lovers." Fancy talk indeed! I don't think my girlie heard because she didn't have any idea who he was either.

At that moment his friend came over and said it was time to go and as he dragged him off, he looked over his shoulder at my girlie, making silent promises to her with those puppy dog eyes. She was thrilled and as everyone started leaving for bed she was as lively as a cricket jumping around in the grass.

"Who is he, who is he?" was all she kept saying. "I'll die if I don't find out and I'll just die if you tell me he's already spoken for. He's all mine. No one else can have him." And I was the one who had to break the news to her that he came from that family. I held her hands and I looked into her eyes and I told her. She was aghast. It wasn't what she would have planned either, but there you are. There's no accounting for these things.

"So I'm condemned to love him and hate him at the same time. How could I love someone from the family I'm supposed to hate?" I suppose this *was* confusing and shocking for her. She did want to do what she was supposed to do and be a good daughter. But suddenly she was looking at a new kind of loyalty, a new connection, a new path to take if she was going to follow her heart. She was bewildered. I took her hand and led her to her room as she sighed and moaned, all the while smiling the simpering smile of the besotted.

Can there really be such a thing as love at first sight? I had just seen it happen—the thunderbolt out of the blue. But was this really love? If not, then what was it, the stirring of the sexual hotpot? The sparking of the sexual fire? How does it happen? If it is not this then what is love? I would say it was all this and more. Real love comes of knowledge. How can you love someone you don't know? My husband, God rest his soul, was my best friend. The feeling of love I had with him was like putting on a warm pair of old slippers. It was comfortable. It was safe and it was reliable. The feeling I was seeing in my girlie right now was exciting. It was dangerous and it was unexpected. When the breathless excitement dies away, then what is left? It should be the warm slippers and that baggy old jumper, but my girlie had no thought for the future that night. She was in the passion of the moment and how I envied her.

I was immensely disappointed with the way things went that evening. This was supposed to be our great triumph, a showcase of our generosity and a celebration of our plans for the future of our beautiful daughter. Instead the whole occasion was marred by what should really have been a trifling incident between my nephew and some uninvited guests. What a fine young man my nephew was and so solicitous of the family's good name. He was a proud young gentleman and I mean that in the best possible sense. He was proud of our reputation, of our position in society and of our nobility both of antecedence and character. He was proud and loyal and I could not have asked more of him if he were my own son. In many ways he was a son to me. He was the son I never had, so he was the compensation for my misery of never having produced a male heir for my husband.

My husband was such a magnanimous host, welcoming all the revellers, one and all, whoever they might be. He sought only to display his generosity of spirit to all. It was my nephew who recognised the voice of one of those gatecrashers, hiding in a corner. It was that boy, the son of our rivals, a family with whom all of our dealings had been unpleasant. He was there with his cohorts, slipping in to take advantage of our munificence. It should really have been of no consequence, although I shared my nephew's irritation. How dare they! What impudence! I found myself shaking my head at their gall. My nephew however was not one to let things go. When he pointed the intruder out to his uncle, my husband reacted with the joviality and bigheartedness that is typical of him in general and even more so on this special occasion. He told our nephew to calm down, that it was fine with him if the boy had joined the party. He didn't want the appearance of any unseemliness on our part. He told him just to smile and be polite. We would remain benevolent hosts. We would remain in the right. When my nephew objected in his righteousness, my husband told him that he would just have to put up with it. He spoke harshly to the boy who took it badly and stormed off, feeling outraged by the intrusion and demeaned by his uncle's reproof. I would have liked to have spoken up for the boy. He was only concerned about this inconsiderate infringement on our generous hospitality. As far as he was concerned it was a violation of our welcome.

I lost sight of the intruder after that. Had I known what he was up to I would have paid more attention, but at the time I thought he was of no real consequence. Now I wonder why he had come in the first place. Was it his intention to steal away our daughter from us? Did he know that we were planning to marry her off and deliberately come to undermine our plans? Had he heard of her beauty and come to inspect her for himself? Or was he just an opportunist with no real plans other than general mischief? I don't know and I never shall. I only wish I had paid more attention.

My other source of disappointment that night was the fact that my daughter's would-be suitor seemed not to arouse her interest at all. She was polite enough, but I had hoped to catch her stealing coy glances at him and giving him small encouragements with her eyes and her smiles. It was not to be. For much of the evening I couldn't even see her among all the guests. When it grew late I wasn't even sure where she was and had to send the nurse to call her for me. What was the woman thinking to let that boy speak to her, for he certainly must have done so? Perhaps they had already been meeting in secret. Otherwise it could not all have come about so quickly. Not even the young can be that reckless. I have so many regrets now. I could have been more insistent that she spend time with the man we had chosen for her. The purpose of the event had been for her to meet him, but she hardly gave him a glance the entire evening. I should have been more insistent. I had thought that by hanging back I would not make her feel pressured and we didn't want anything to get in the way of the match going forward, even if it were not immediately. Oh, I shall regret my attempt at discretion forever.

Four

I pushed her back to her room as quickly as I could, considering her dreamy intent on dawdling. Her feet sort of tripped over each other as I nudged her along. It seemed like I ought to get her behind closed doors before anyone else noticed that look on her face. We didn't need the complication of the master or the mistress getting wind of this.

"That's enough of that nonsense," I told her. "You'll have the whole household knowing what you've been up to."

"And so what if they *do* know. I'm not ashamed of being in love."

"Well love is one thing, but we don't need everyone sharing the secret now, do we?"

"And why should it be a secret if I'm in love?"

"Well a secret is one thing, but you don't have to go alerting the whole neighbourhood like an overly enthusiastic town crier."

"Ah …" and her sigh of replete contentment reverberated around the room. There's no reasoning with someone in that first flush of heartstopping ecstasy. I echoed her sigh, but mine was more of resigned scepticism. The sighs of innocence and experience.

"Ah, he was so wonderful," she cooed.

"Wonderful, my arse. He's a troublemaker of the first order and no good is going to come out of this."

"How can you say that? You don't know him like I do."

"Know him!" I rolled my eyes heavenward. It was my turn to sigh. "I don't need to 'know' him to know he's a jumped-up, smooth-talking, presumptuous little flatterer who could talk the hind leg off a donkey."

"How do *you* know?" she whined. "He's a poet and a dreamer."

"Well let him dream on, that's what I say." Then I saw the hurt in her eyes and I laughed, taking hold of her and drawing her to me. "Let him go to dreamland and meet you there, my girlie. It's time for bed."

"Bed! You must be crazy. There's no way I'm going to bed now. There's no way I could sleep for thinking of him." Didn't I say we'd be up till dawn! She stopped suddenly, listening.

"Did you hear something?" she said hurriedly. When I tried to answer she shushed me so she could listen. "It must be him. He's come." And she rushed over to the window, looking out into the night. Well, blow me, if she wasn't right. It *was* him: that boy, Mr. Poetry and Flowers himself, right under her window, just waiting for a glimpse of her. She looked out into the darkness and we both knew he was there, although she didn't see where he was straight away. He was lurking under the balcony like a thief in the night, come to steal my girlie's heart.

I tried not to listen. After all it wasn't my business what passed between them and I didn't want to be a busybody and a killjoy. But I couldn't help hearing, really I couldn't and to tell you the truth I really didn't know quite where to put myself. Those two only had ears and eyes for each other and I just turned into a fly on the wall. And what fancy words that boy had for her. He went on and on about how she was sunlight in the darkness and her eyes were the stars and oh, the heavenly beauty, shining bright as day to make the birds sing even though it was night time. And she stood there on the balcony calling to him, saying they should forget their own names so they could be together. And then *she* went all poetic and all. And I never even knew she had it in her.

"What does a name matter?" she cooed. She wittered on about how a rose still has a lovely smell if you call it something else. (Yes and you-know-what stinks and all.) She said he could get rid of his name; he'd be just perfect to her. Well that set him right off. All he wanted was for her to call him "her love". Well, it didn't look like there was much doubt about that. It's enough to make you roll your eyes all the way back into your head. She was all aflutter, wanting to know how he got there over those high walls into the garden. He told her how love has wings and can fly over walls. (It just has boots and can climb, I reckon.) Then my girlie went all dramatic and said her family shouldn't find him there or they'd kill him. Well that wasn't going to scare *him*—he was a victim of her beautiful eyes that had pierced him right through and he'd rather be killed as long as she loved him than be condemned to live to a ripe old age without her love. Oh my! She wanted to know how he found her and he told her he was guided by love. He'd go to the ends of the earth to find her. What pretty words indeed!

Of course she fell for him and she didn't hold anything back, the darkness hiding her blushes. She was bold enough to ask him to tell her if he loved her. She already knew what his answer would be. If he loved her he would say so and if he didn't truly love her, he would still say that he did. And she would believe him anyway. Her voice was so full of the dizziness of excitement that I hardly knew her. I was right—my girlie really was lost. She was his completely. She was breathless, as if she could hear her own heart beating and her words of love were whispered with an intensity that it pains me to recall. So innocent and so vulnerable. My heart ached for losing her to the grown up world and for fear that she would be hurt in giving herself so completely. She seemed to worry that she was laying herself bare, so to speak, too quickly, that she was being too forward, but she just couldn't help herself. Wasn't this every girl's dream, hearing words of love from a stranger in the night? He was swearing by the moon that he loved her, but she thought the moon was too fickle, changing all the time through the month. She's a clever one my girlie. She started to say goodnight and the next thing I knew that boy was talking about exchanging vows of love. And they'd only known each other five minutes!

Was I judging him too harshly? I understand how she would believe every word. Who wouldn't fall in love with such expressions of tender devotion? We are all in love with love. For her it was the first time and it was completely irresistible. But what about him? I know it wasn't the first time he had spoken words of love, but here was the response he had longed for. So for him too this was in a sense a first time and it was so beautiful. Even so, it was time to call her in from her folly.

"Girlie," I called. "My girlie, come in from that balcony." I did my best to sound firm and stern. She said her hurried goodbyes and came in. *I* could see the blushes. She was flushed with joy, like she'd burst.

"It's him," she said. "Out there. He came. He came to me." And her hand gestured out into the night in a circling movement. She spun around, hugging herself as if she was about to swoon. I clucked and tutted, but I couldn't help an indulgent smile. What joy to see her this happy. Then before I could say a word she was out there again, leaning out, just to be near him and giving him the eyeballs of mush. I was flabbergasted to hear what she came out with next.

"Say you'll marry me," she said and she was telling him she'd send someone to him tomorrow to arrange where and when they'd tie the knot. What? Blimey, this girl really was sick with love. Oh throw caution down the drain, show your true colours and let him use you like a dishrag. That's what *I* was thinking. And him! He couldn't believe his luck, I'm sure. He was getting it handed to him on a plate!

"Girlie!" Did I sound harsh? I had to get her inside before she threw herself off the balcony into his arms.

"I'm coming, I'm coming, I'm coming." But then she turned back to him.

"Girlie!" I had to do *something* for goodness' sake. And she told him that if he wasn't serious about it then he should just leave her to her misery, but she would send someone tomorrow.

"A thousand goodnights," I heard her throw to him as she scurried back inside. (It wasn't my hundred kisses she'd want that night!) She came tripping in with the thrill of it bursting from her eyes. A moment later she was out there again calling him back.

"What time tomorrow?" He answered nine o'clock. That seemed like an eternity to her, but it seemed way too soon to me. When was I going to get my beauty sleep? The night would be over before we even got to our beds. She just didn't want to say goodbye. She kept forgetting what she was going to say, then realising that he'd stay longer, waiting for her to remember, she just kept on forgetting! She finally managed to tear herself away, wallowing in the joy of her love and the exquisite misery of saying goodbye to him.

She finally swayed dreamily back into the room, the guileless grin of the lovelorn on her bemused face. My little cherub.

"Come here, girlie," I clucked and I folded her into my arms. Well, she certainly wasn't ready for bed. She just wanted to go over it all again, over and over, reliving the moment. I helped her undress and brushed her lovely blond hair just like I did when she was a little girl, but tonight was nothing like when she was a little girl.

"Oh why does he have to be from that family?" There was a wee bit of the little girl in that, stamping her foot to get what she wants. "Why wasn't *he* the one who was chosen for me? He's the one who is destined for me."

"We don't always get to choose in life and we can't choose our destiny. We can choose to accept it or we can choose to be rebellious." I know she wasn't really listening to me and I don't think she was really talking to me either, more to herself, like a running commentary on her thoughts.

"I'd give up my name for him," she continued.

"Well, that's not an option," I muttered, but she wasn't listening. In one ear and out the other!

"If we could both just give up our names … But there's nothing really in a name anyway. It's not what you *are*. It's not the essence of you. It's just a big stumbling block, a barrier that other people would put up between us. But we can get over that, just like he got over the wall tonight because we had to be together." There was plenty of truth in this, but the names were still there, hanging like a threatening thundercloud, come to spoil a picnic. "He would do anything for me. He said he would go anywhere for me. He would die for me."

"Well, let's hope that won't be necessary," I said, smiling a rueful smile. She smiled back at me, brimming over with happiness.

"I know that he loves me. That is all I need. It's like a binding contract that we made tonight."

"Oh, the ties that bind," I mused.

"Love binds tighter than family ties," she answered and I knew she was right. This is a union she was choosing to make, not something that she had grown up with or had been urged upon her. It was the act of choice itself that made it so special and so irresistible to her. What can I say? She just couldn't help herself.

"It was when he talked about exchanging faithful vows that I knew it was the real thing. He loves me. He means it. He said so."

"Hmm," I responded. I wondered how many times he had said it before. Did he mean it then? Did he mean it now? Did he only mean it because *she* meant it? Did it matter? Shouldn't she just lie back and enjoy it? Your first love only comes along once in a lifetime, after all. I wanted her to seize the moment and live it to the full. The future didn't matter. If he hurt her she would survive. She would get married to the wonderful husband the master and the mistress had chosen for her and all would be well. But in the meantime she'd drink up the draught of first love, she'd knock it back in one huge gulp and then she'd stagger around drunk as a skunk for as long as it lasted. The hangover would be worth it!

"He said so," she repeated. "He said so. Don't you know he loves me?"

"I know that *you* love *him*. You're drunk with love my girlie. Your cup runneth over." We both giggled. I loved this intimacy with her. I loved the complicity. We were like two giggling schoolgirls, sharing secrets. Yes, my reason was telling me that no good was going to come of it, but even though I wasn't taken in by him for a minute, somehow I couldn't help myself any more than she could. I was going to help her, even though I thought he was a rat. I didn't like him and I didn't trust him any more than a thief in the night. And I knew he was that.

"So I know I can be his forever. I know he means it. That means we can be married and our families will just have to get used to it because by the time they find out we'll belong to each other and there's nothing they can do about it."

"Yes, my girlie, you'll be all hitched up and no man can put you asunder."

"To love and to cherish"

"For richer, for poorer."

"Till death do us part."

We each sighed our own sighs once again.

"It's like giving a gift being in love," she said. "It makes me feel so generous, like I'm giving myself all the time and it doesn't matter how much I give him, there's always more of me to give." If only he knew the value of that gift, I thought to myself. If only he would treasure it and protect it to keep it intact. I feared he would eventually toss it aside to shatter into a thousand pieces that couldn't be put back together.

"I just couldn't say goodnight."

"You said it a thousand times."

"Well, that was because I didn't really want it to be goodnight. I just wanted to keep on talking to him."

There was a pause. I think I must have yawned.

"Love makes life worth living," she said slowly. "This is what it's all about. Now I'm alive. Now I'm really living."

"And what were you doing before? Waiting in your cocoon like a butterfly?"

She beamed. "Yes, that's it. Now I have spread my wings and I'm going to fly away with him."

I smiled to myself and without even realising that I was saying it aloud I heard my own voice sighing, "Enjoy it while it lasts, girlie. Enjoy it while it lasts."

Before I went to bed that night I sought out my poor nephew to console and commiserate with him. I found him pacing his room in sullen resolve, silently punching the palm of his hand with a grim expression on his face. At first he was unwilling to talk to me, he was so angry and surly. I stood quietly in the doorway and waited for him to be ready to speak.

Finally he shared his thoughts with me. He felt humiliated and was struggling with a way to channel his anger. He did not want to admit that some of his resentment was directed at my husband and sought to blame it all on that dreadful boy. I encouraged him in this. After all, his uncle was a well-meaning man. He meant not to put down our nephew, only to diffuse the situation with as little fuss as possible. I could understand this. Yes, it was important to keep up appearances and the less fuss there was the better.

My nephew began to rant about the impudence of the boy and his bunch of wayward friends. I agreed with everything he said, not only so that he wouldn't blame his uncle, but because I thought he was absolutely right about everything. He said that they were only there to take advantage of our largesse, to get some free food and drink and to have a good laugh at our expense. Once they knew that he had recognised them and my husband had put him in his place, they no doubt thought that they had somehow won a moral victory, that they had scored points against him—and it was my husband who had awarded them that victory. Well of course he was feeling humiliated. His pacing became faster and he started to raise his voice.

"They'll pay for this," he was saying over and over again, hitting his palm with his other clenched fist. "Especially that little ringleader. He thinks he's something special, walking in here like he owns the place and I can't do a thing about it. Well, we'll see about that." He almost spat out these last words.

"Yes," I said, touching his shoulder. He pulled away violently. He was trembling as he met my eyes.

"Don't you worry," I said. "He'll get what's coming to him."

"Oh, I'll make sure of that," he answered in almost a growl. "I'll make sure of that."

I smiled at him, but his expression didn't change. I shuddered. Was it cold all of a sudden or was it just the coldness in his heart? It never occurred to me at that moment that my nephew might be in danger himself from his own bravado. Afterwards I was left to remember that I had egged him on. Fate is so cruel.

As I left his room I went to find my husband who was probably still up. As I passed the passageway to my daughter's room I noticed that there was a light visible under her door. So she was still awake too. The whole household was awake in one sort of turmoil or another. I went to her door and was about to knock. I took in my breath to say something and as I did so I heard the nurse's voice calling to her. So she was there with her. I had no desire to talk to the woman, so I caught my breath and walked away from the door without knocking. I would speak to her in the morning.

My husband was still up, sipping on a full glass of deep red wine. He was sighing, satisfied with his evening's triumph. When I said that I had hoped to see the girl more interested in her suitor he just laughed at me.

"She's young," he said indulgently. "She'll come around to the idea. What is there not to like about him?"

I looked at him with perhaps a slightly more than dubious smile. He laughed again.

"You'll see." He nodded to himself, staring into his wine. "She'll come around and she'll be grateful. What's not to like?"

"Yes, you're right of course," I said, slowly nodding my head, "But I can't help but be disappointed. I had hoped she would not be able to resist his charms once she took a look at him. He's such a fine looking young man and so suave and debonair. I had hoped that she'd be excited about the match."

"She will be, she will be," he responded. "Once we set the date she'll be thrilled. She'll get used to the idea and I must say, I like it more the more I think about it. I think we'll have a wedding soon, my dear. Don't you fret." He glanced at me as he took another sip of his wine and I had to smile.

"You're right as usual," I said. "Things will work out soon enough." But I sighed as I said this. I just couldn't shake off the feeling of disappointment. If only this had remained the worst of our troubles. Perhaps I was discomfited by that boy's behaviour or my nephew's humiliation. Whatever it was that was troubling me, it was still with me as I said goodnight. Perhaps things would seem better in the morning. A good night's sleep has a way of healing many troubles and I had no reason to think that this would be any different. My husband was confident that all was well and he was usually right about things. He was in charge and I could feel secure that he would take care of things. Of course the idea of this marriage would grow on my daughter. Of course she would be grateful for her father's choice. Of course.

Five

The next morning I half expected everything to have gone back to the way it was before, as if it had all been a dream, but as soon as my girlie woke up, I knew that nothing was going to go back to the way it was before any time soon. This was a new day and a new reality. Although nothing had really happened, nothing was ever going to be the same again. It was like losing your virginity. You could put the whole thing on one side, think about something else, pretend it never happened, but you could never change the fact that it *did* happen. It's like breaking an ornament. You could glue the pieces back together, but you'd always see the join.

She leapt out of bed like a jack-in-a-box and ran to the window, just to be near where he had been. Somehow she seemed to expect everything to carry on exactly where it had left off. Lover boy was still there in her mind, whispering sweet nothings under her window all night long. I can only guess at what her dreams had been!

She was all in a tizzy, wanting me to go and find him and make arrangements for them to get married. Oh my, she was really serious. I didn't think for a moment that he had any intention of going through with it. After all, I knew he was a bit fickle where women were concerned: one minute all hot and bothered over one girl and the next minute it would be someone else altogether. Last night it was my girlie. Who knows what he would be thinking today! It all depended which way the wind was blowing for all I could see. I think he liked the drama of it, the forbidden fruit thing. He probably wouldn't have looked at her twice if she'd been introduced to him as his betrothed.

She kept nagging and nagging me to get off my rear end, not that she put it quite like that. I was supposed to meet him at nine o'clock. It was barely the crack of dawn and she was trying to shove me out the door. I certainly wasn't going to go without my breakfast and I suggested that she shouldn't either. Of course her stomach was the last thing on her mind and she continued to nag instead of eating. It is astonishing how those in love can live on thin air, although I have to say that it never did anything to *my* appetite.

I decided not to go alone. I thought it probably wouldn't look proper for a woman on her own to approach a young gentleman, so I dragged a servant lad with me. As we walked I thought about what had happened. Now, what was the state of things at that point? The lad kept interrupting my thoughts with his silly wittering. Now, where was I? Oh yes, the state of things. Well, the way I saw it, my girlie had fallen A over T for a good-looking, overly-romantic young cad who was good with words, but probably didn't mean any of them. I strongly disapproved, yet here I was, doing her bidding because I couldn't refuse her anything. No matter, she was going to come back to earth with an almighty bump and I would make sure I would be there to dry her tears and pick up the pieces. You can't say fairer than that. That seemed to me to be the most likely outcome at the time. I expected that he wouldn't even speak to me this morning, in the cold light of day so to speak. What if I didn't even find him, if he was playing hard to get or had already decided that this wasn't such a good idea? What if he pretended he didn't even know her? Suppose he sent me packing without a word for her? What would I say to her? How could I soften the blow? Should I even try to soften the blow? Maybe it would be better just to let her suffer the disappointment. Would it be better for her to be angry with him or with me?

I really wasn't too sure where I was going to find him. We walked over to his family's neighbouring estate and waited around near the gate house for a while, but no one was coming or going. The lad wanted to know what we were doing there, who we were waiting for. I told him to mind his own beeswax. He was just there to keep me company is what I told him, so he should just keep his trap shut and remember that no one needed to know what we had been doing. He said no one was going to know because he didn't know himself, the cheeky little duffer. Then we walked on into Great Stonewick. No luck there either and the lad was whining and moaning and saying he wanted to go home. He wasn't the only one. We started to head off towards home when I spotted that boy with two of his pals. I think one of them was related to him, but I didn't know how, a cousin or something. Well, it wasn't any of my business anyway.

We went over and it wasn't easy to start a conversation, I can tell you. Well, what do you say? He and his friends, especially one of them, not the cousin, the other one, started taking the mickey out of us as soon as I opened my mouth.

"Good morning," I started to say.

"Good afternoon, you mean," sneered the nasty one. "It's gone noon, your ladyship."

They all laughed. Cheeky blighter, I thought to myself.

"What a wanker," whispered the young lad behind me. I smiled.

"Get away with you," I said, as dignified as I could muster. "Just who do you think you are?" He clearly thought he was the sherry in the trifle.

"I'm looking for a certain young gentleman," I said, giving that boy a meaningful look.

"I'm pretty young," he shot back. "And I'm certainly a gentleman. You could do worse."

"Well, thank heavens for small mercies." He grinned. His haughty friend tried to butt in with some snide comment, but I ignored him. "I'd like an undercover word with you if you don't mind, young sir."

"Ooh," said the cousin. "She wants to get you under the covers!" Then the nasty one joined in. "Wooh! A bit of slap and tickle with a right old slapper." He started singing some rude song, then he and the cousin said they were off. They darted away, nearly wetting themselves with laughter and we were left alone with that boy.

"And who was that foul-mouthed so-and-so?" I asked, trying to sound as posh and dignified as I could.

"Oh he's quite a gentleman, I assure you." And he smirked as he said it. "He's all talk. Take no notice."

"I'd like to put him across my knee and teach him a lesson. And you," I said, poking the lad I'd brought with me. "You just stood there and let him insult me."

"What a wanker," he said out loud. "Don't worry, I wouldn't let anyone take advantage of you."

"I should hope not, even if he *is* all mouth and no trousers. Well, that's enough about him. I came to be the messenger for my girlie, so it's time to get down to business." Well, that's what I'd come for, to get down to business with that boy, but before I did I had to issue him a warning. I wanted him to know who he was dealing with.

"You'd better not be trifling with her or leading her a merry dance," I said, thrusting my chin out and trying to make myself look a little bit taller. "That would be a low down bastardly thing to do for sure and I'm not going to stand for it, what with her being so young and vulnerable and all."

He started swearing to me (not at me) and then he said, "Here's my proposition." Well, that *did* help me feel a little better and I told him so.

"A proposition sounds promising enough," I said, "and she'd be overjoyed to hear it."

"Stop wittering on," he interrupted. "I haven't told you yet what I want you to say to her."

"Well your proposition sounds very gentlemanly," I told him. And then he got down to the nub of it. He said to tell her to come down to see that vicar chappy that very afternoon so they could get hitched. The vicar kept himself locked away in a little cottage just outside Little Stonewick, so it would be very discreet. Well fancy that! He was *talking* about going through with it at least. Then he tried to give me a tip for my trouble. What an insult! As if I was no more than a common servant. I ask you, what did she see in him?

Then he told me that he wanted me to wait down by the churchyard wall and he would send someone with a rope ladder, so he could come to my girlie in secret that night. Then they could be together as man and wife, like. It didn't seem right to me that he would want to do that in secret if they were really married. How long did he mean to keep it a secret and why? Would it turn out that he was just using her after all? Well if that was going to be the way it would turn out, then she would have loved and learned. All I could do was warn her, but I already knew she wasn't going to pay any attention to me.

"Well, I just need to know if you're sending someone trustworthy," I said with dignity.

"Of course he'll be trustworthy."

"Well, so much the better," I returned, "My girlie being such a lovely lady and all. And what a beautiful child she was and cute as a button, bright as a button too." (And why would a button be cute, I've always wondered?)

"She's got another suitor, you know," I told him. I paused for effect and to see what he'd say, but he didn't say anything, so I went on, "And he's a fine and a handsome one too. He's much better looking in my opinion, a really good catch, but she'll have none of him since she set eyes on you." I was prattling on again and he couldn't be bothered to hang around and listen. He wasn't polite enough. He sent his wishes to my girlie and off he strode, leaving us there to get on with our business. Well, I never. That just confirmed my opinion of him.

The whole affair was doomed as far as I could see. He wasn't fit to lick her boots, but she wasn't going to see it. She was all sighs and butterflies. No wonder they say love is blind. She just shut her eyes to the real world and wouldn't have listened to me whatever I'd said.

The next morning everyone in the household must have slept late after all the excitement of the night before. I was eager to speak to my daughter, to see what she thought about the festivities and about the special guest we had welcomed for her to meet. Perhaps I could plant a seed of favour on his behalf. Then he would slowly grow on her and their relationship could ripen in the fullness of time. I fervently hoped for this for her. Her father was going to agree to the match. He had told the young man as much. It seemed to me that if the idea could grow on her, then so much the better and the future would be bright for us all. There was no question of her refusing what her father had chosen for her.

I went to her room and knocked. She leaped up and ran to the door to greet me. When I saw her I could see she was flushed with excitement, although I could tell that it hadn't been me that she had expected to see right at that moment. Her eyes were bright and she seemed agitated. My first thought was that perhaps I had been wrong. Perhaps she had taken a fancy to the young man after all. Well, I would have been glad of it.

"So, girl," I said, smiling at her. "How did you enjoy our ball, last night? Was it not all you had hoped for?"

"Oh yes," she enthused. "It was wonderful." She looked down coyly. My, it seemed that I had misjudged the situation after all.

"And did you enjoy the company?" I gave her a sideways glance, trying to suppress my curiosity, but I wanted her to speak to me of him.

"Oh yes," she repeated. "Oh yes, oh yes!"

Well, that's good news, I thought.

"Well, that's good news," I said. I was amazed. This was a far better reaction than I had expected and she had certainly hidden it well the night before.

"And..." I hesitated. "And was there anyone in particular that you were glad to meet?" I said as casually as I could muster.

"Oh yes," she bleated again, looking off into the distance. There was no mistaking that flush. I had definitely misjudged the situation ... or so I thought.

"So..." I tried to catch her eye. "So what did you think? Did you like him?"

"Yes," she gushed. "Yes, yes, yes. He's handsome and..."

I looked at her expectantly.

"He's perfect."

I smiled at her indulgently.

"Nobody's perfect." I smiled.

"Why not?" she countered. I couldn't help but grin.

"They don't have to be. Just good and honest and reasonably well off is good enough."

She pouted.

"Maybe," she said, "but perfect is better." She smiled a lovely, radiant smile and I was aware of her beauty. How naive she was and how delightful I found it, despite the fact that it was puzzling to me. It was so unexpected after what I had seen last night. I hadn't spotted a single glance exchanged between the two of them. Well, puzzling or not, it was still delightful and I was more than happy to accept this unexpected turn of events.

"Well, in that case," I conjectured, "How about I talk to your father and see if we can hurry things along a bit? He'd be glad to know of your eagerness and I think he might be persuaded to make things happen a little sooner."

"Oh!" was all she replied, wide eyed and I laughed at her bemusement. There was something tremendously appealing about the innocence she displayed and I felt a rush of affection for this naive young girl I had brought into the world. Here she was, already on the threshold of matrimony and thrilled at the prospect. It was way more than I could have hoped for.

What was it realistic to hope for? I hoped that she would marry at a good age and safely deliver a number of children, including male heirs. This way she would achieve more than I had. I think it is reasonable to hope that one's children will do better in life than one has oneself. I hoped that she would have a good marriage to a good and honourable man. What do I mean by a good marriage? I mean that she would be well provided for, that she would live comfortably, I hoped more comfortably than I, although I am satisfied enough with my lot. I hoped that she would be content, that she would be happy. And what is happiness? I think it is a matter of expec-

tations. *If your expectations are realistic, then you can be happy. If you set your expectations too high, if you are a dreamer hoping for something you can never achieve, then you will never be happy, but always yearning for what you can't have.* What I had hoped for for my daughter was merely that she would anticipate only what would be reasonable considering her circumstances and that she would consequently not have to spend her life craving and longing for something unattainable. And what about love in her marriage? Should that be part of her expectations? Is that unreasonable? I would say that happiness in marriage is based more on respect and esteem than on what some might call love. When I had asked her the day before if she could love the man, I meant the kind of love that is based on respect, the kind that is earned by behaving with integrity. A passionate physical love would be a nice bonus, but it is not likely to last. Then what? When the fiery passion of love has burnt itself out, then you can remain happy if you still have respect. This is the foundation of a marriage. It has worked well for me and that is what I had hoped would work for her too.

I looked at my daughter. I could see the glow of the adolescent love that she was experiencing and thought that this was icing on the cake. We had chosen a fine man for her. If she felt love for him then this was good. I smiled at her. At this moment I felt more warmth than I had ever felt for her and perhaps a tinge of envy too for the joy she was experiencing.

"All will be well, girl," I said and I had a sudden unexpected urge to stroke her hair, but she pulled away from my touch. "I shall speak to your father and we'll see what we can arrange for you."

"Thank you," she whispered. "Thank you," she repeated, this time barely audibly.

Six

When we finally got back to my girlie, she was pacing the room.

"Where've you been?" she whined. "I've been wondering where on earth you could have got to."

"It's all very well for you to talk," I countered. "You weren't the one who was traipsing around all over the countryside looking for him." You should have seen her face light up when I mentioned him. She wanted to talk in private, so I sent the lad off to busy himself with something. He asked what he should busy himself with and I said how should I know what lads busied themselves with, but it was time to be doing it and somewhere else than where my girlie and I were having our private conversation.

"Oh," was all he said as he slunk off. "I'll do that then."

"Well, what news do you have for me?" She was almost bursting to know. "You don't look too happy? Is it bad news? If it's bad news, then break it to me gently. If it's good news, then don't spoil it by being such a sourpuss. Tell me which is it? Is it good or bad?" Lordy, I could hardly get a word in edge ways.

"Just let me sit down a minute, I'm all tuckered out."

"Tell me, tell me, tell me!" I smiled to myself with wicked enjoyment. Oh what fun it was to keep her in suspense.

"Hold on a minute," I said. "Have you got no patience at all? I'm all out of breath with running all over the place for you. Now just hold on."

"If you're out of breath then why are you wasting it on telling me how worn out you are? Get on with it. Just tell me, is it good or bad?"

"Why do you need to know what I have to say? You already made your choice and I'm buggered if I know why you've chosen this one.

He's rude as they come and as for looks, he's not a patch on your intended."

"But *he's* my intended. He's the one I intend to marry. What did he say? What did he say about getting married?"

"Ooh, do I have a headache! My head aches and my back aches from all the running around you've had me do today. Lordy, I need a rest."

"Well, I'm sorry if you're out of sorts, but I need to know. What did he say? What did my love say to you?"

"Well …" (Oh how I was enjoying keeping her on tenterhooks) "Your wonderful love, like the true gentleman that he is, very polite, honest as the day is long, kind, handsome (though not as handsome as some) and I'd like to be able to say virtuous …" I paused dramatically. "Where is her ladyship?"

"Her ladyship? I think she's in the house somewhere. What does it matter where she is? You were talking about my love, the gentleman, the honest, kind and virtuous gentleman …"

"Yes, have you got something to soothe my aching bones? You know, you can take care of your own messages from now on."

"This is driving me mad. Tell me what he said!"

"Well," I said

"Well?" she said.

"Well …" I repeated.

"Well, go on." You should have seen her face. It was a picture. I couldn't keep her in suspense any longer, even though it was such fun.

"Well, can you get away at some point today?" I grinned slyly.

"Yes, yes, yes!"

"Well, if you go to the vicarage in the village, you know, then you'll find not only the vicar, but a groom there, waiting to make you his bride."

You should have seen the colour rise in her cheeks. Oh, the thrill of it. It was joy to me to see the elation on that face. She hugged me, she squealed and her eyes danced with the bliss of the moment. I was glad to be the one to bring her such joy, even though I had such forebodings for the outcome. She was *my* joy. We hugged and she actually jumped up and down with delight. It was worth everything to share this moment with her.

What is the difference between adolescent love and the kind of love felt by those of us with a few more years under our belts? Is it the same thing? Just more intense? More urgent? Or is it something completely different? Is it based on something real or something we just imagine, more to do with the perfect person we want to meet like in the stories? Is the only difference that when we're older we don't expect so much, because we have already been disappointed? We've already loved and learned. I said I thought that nobody (except my girlie) really expects to love just one person in their lifetime. But maybe that's what we all expect until we learn by experience that it's not the case. I just don't know.

Maybe that first love *is* something different. It's like the first time you see a sunset. It's different because it's new and it's like nothing you've ever felt before. Like what I said about a baby's smile. Young love is such a physical thing. You feel it all over like a tingling that's thrilling and full of anticipation. When you walk in the street you think you see him everywhere. Suddenly everyone looks like the one you love because he is all you are thinking of. I remember when I was her age my father used to laugh at me when I talked of love. He said I didn't know what it meant, but I think I just didn't know what it meant to him.

And what did it mean to my girlie right now? It meant the breathless excitement. It meant the impatience to be next to him: to be next to him at the altar, to be next to him in bed, just to be next to him, to drink him in. He was all she could think of, all she needed and there was no thought of tomorrow. Well, of course there was no thought of tomorrow. Tomorrow just didn't exist for her.

I'm sure she just didn't have room in her thoughts for the master and the mistress. She just didn't have any plans for what she would say to them. Wasn't it just yesterday that she told them she had never thought about love and marriage? I suppose it would seem to them that she had a lot of explaining to do, not that there *was* any explanation, other than that thunderbolt out of the blue. But something tells me they wouldn't be interested in any kind of explanations anyway. As far as they were concerned, they were in charge of whoever it would be that she would love and marry. I suppose *they* didn't really know the meaning of it either. Had they had a choice to love and to marry? Maybe they would say that they did. They had the choice to love the person they married, even if they couldn't marry the person they loved. And they would expect that of her too—to love the man of their choice.

After my little interview with my daughter I went straight to my husband to share with him the good news that he had been right. It was a good match and she was surely going to agree happily to it.

I found him alone, poring over his accounts as he so often does. He was humming to himself as he studied the books, no doubt in self satisfaction. He had pulled off rather a fine coup and had demonstrated the generosity of spirit and flawless character of our excellent family. As I stood in the doorway I felt a pang of affection for him in his magnanimity. I did love him for his wisdom, for his good judgment and for his single-mindedness when it came to matters of the family's honour. It was a well-worn love that would remain with us as we grew older. It was a love born of the realistic expectation I had that he would faithfully consider our reputation as a couple and would always act with decency and respect towards me. I would always be comfortable with him, both materially and morally. I could ask for no more and so I was happy.

"Well it would seem you were right," I began.

"Right?" he said. "Right about what?"

"About our daughter," was my simple reply.

"And in what capacity have I been right?" he went on.

"In choosing a man that she can love."

"And how do you know this?" he asked, frowning a little in case he was deceived in my meaning.

"I have spoken to her and she says that he is perfect. You should have seen how excited she was."

He frowned again and looked at me in an almost suspicious way.

"But that was not your impression last night," he said. "What has changed?"

I shook my head. After all, I was as surprised as he was.

"Perhaps we were just not watching her closely enough last night," I said, "We were too busy hosting and smiling at our guests. The nurse took her off to bed before I could even take a look at her." This was indeed so. I remember looking around for her at the end of the evening and watching as the nurse almost dragged her off up the stairs without even a goodnight.

"Well, well," he said, sitting down and leaning against the back of his chair. "Who would have thought it? Who would have thought it?"

"Who, indeed?" I said with a shrug. "But no matter. This morning she was flushed with excitement at the thought of him and I think we should waste no time in letting him know that she has spoken favourably of the prospect of becoming his bride. Perhaps we should waste no time in concluding the arrangements."

"I told him yesterday that I wasn't sure I was ready to part with her. She is so young. But I encouraged him and if she is willing, then I see no reason to delay for too long. We don't want her changing her mind now, do we?" He laughed heartily as he said this. "No, we can't have her changing her mind. That would be far too embarrassing!"

He was nodding to himself, pleased with the situation as it stood.

"Hmm ...," he mused. "Was it really only yesterday that he spoke to me? How quickly things can happen when the time is right." He continued to nod and chuckle to himself and I found myself smiling indulgently. I too was delighted with the state of matters.

Were we just seeing what we wanted to see? Is that always the way of things? Does one always close one's eyes to what one does not want to see? But there was no other explanation evident at the time. She had seemed *indifferent, but now she seemed to have changed her mind. The truth of the matter was far more unlikely, far more bizarre. Of course I was willing to accept the explanation that not only was more pleasant to me, but was also the only rational possibility. Yes, it was surprising, even bewildering, but then where would one find more fickleness than in the heart of a young girl?*

Seven

We both went our separate ways. She ran off up the path to meet that boy, so that he could make her his bride. At the same time I went on my errand. I went down to the churchyard wall to wait for the man with the rope ladder, so I could bring it back to the house, and they could spend the night together, my girlie and that boy, as newlyweds, in secret. I still didn't like all the secrecy, all this cloak and dagger nonsense. It was almost as if he wanted to turn the whole thing into a romantic game. Would this be a real marriage? The till-death-do-us-part kind? If the vicar was doing it, wouldn't he say it was holy matrimony? Those whom God has joined and all that? He was a man of God. Wouldn't he know what he was doing? I still wasn't sure at all whether this was really happening or not. What if he chickened out at the last minute? What if the vicar wouldn't really do it without their parents' consent?

I waited for ages, thinking about my girlie and what she was doing. Maybe this was all just a cruel joke. Maybe the messenger wasn't going to show up and neither had that boy. Maybe they were watching me from somewhere, that boy and his stinking friends, just to have a good laugh at my expense. I wouldn't put it past them. Well, a laugh at my expense would be one thing, but this would be at my girlie's expense and I'd never be able to forgive that. You can't play with a young girl's heart and soul.

I waited for ages thinking all these dark thoughts, but eventually he did show up and that put me at my ease a little. He seemed like a straight-forward enough bloke and I thanked him for his kindness. I took the rope ladder and lugged it all the way home. The things I do for my girlie, I thought as the heavy ropes cut into my hands, the things I do for my girlie. It must have been quite late by the time I got back.

What I heard when I got back to the house made me stop dead. At first I hoped it was just the below stairs gossip with no truth in it, but one of the kitchen lads was there and saw it with his own eyes. It gave me such a horrible sense of foreboding. Everything had gone terribly wrong and suddenly all the secrecy made dreadful sense. Thank goodness no one *did* know what I'd helped my girlie do. It made me shudder and quiver to think of her in his arms. There had been a fight, you see. Everyone was talking about it. There was a buzz of whisperings and wailings all over the house, but below stairs was where the most gossip always circulated and that was where I heard what happened. My girlie's cousin had gone out looking for that boy after all the trouble of the night before. I think he thought he'd been made a fool of and wanted to teach that boy a lesson he wouldn't forget. Well he didn't find him straight away. Of course he wouldn't have because he was off with the vicar and my girlie, tying the knot, so to speak.

Well, according to what I heard below stairs, while he was in that black mood who should he run into, but that haughty, sneering, nasty piece of work of a friend of my girlie's young man.—the one I had disliked so much, who had teased and ridiculed me in such a spiteful way. They got into a fight, but he wasn't the one he had the quarrel with. According to the gossip when my girlie's new husband showed up (although no one knew he was her husband of course), her cousin challenged him, but he didn't want to fight (just having come from marrying his cousin). Well I suppose he wouldn't want to fight him, would he? Not with being related sort of. But his friend, the nasty one, was just itching for a fight and he went for him. That nasty piece of work got his comeuppance all right. The fight turned quite vicious and he got stabbed. The story was that his friends all thought he was just having them on, pretending to be hurt. That's what he was like, you see. Always making a joke of everything. Always taking the piss. But then they realised. He died cursing the lot of them.

Well, that put lover boy in such a rage for revenge that he fought back and did my poor girlie's cousin in, right there in the street. He was in such a passion. Like I said—quick to love and quick to anger. People saw it. He had no choice but to make himself scarce pretty sharpish. There's no way he could ever show his face around here again. Not ever. He'd be on the run for the rest of his life. All I could think of was what did this mean for my girlie? Was she on the run too? Would anyone find out about what the two of them had done earlier on? I mean the wedding. *I* wasn't going to tell anyone, that was for sure, but I wasn't sure about the vicar. What would *he* do? For me this changed everything. I hadn't liked that boy, not from the very beginning, but now this had happened, how could I let her ruin her life? I just didn't know what to do.

Her ladyship was so distraught to lose her nephew, her brother's son and they were very close. He was like a brother to my girlie. They carried him back to the house and there was blood everywhere. Oh my God, I didn't want her to see it. There was no way that this marriage was going to put an end to the feud now, make no mistake about that. It was the end. Now she was going to have to keep quiet and forget that any of this ever happened. She would just have to do as she was told and marry the nice young man who had been chosen for her. After all, she could do a lot worse and she certainly *would* do a lot worse if anyone found out what she had done. Yes, the gentlemen would all meet and agree on the financial arrangements. When they asked her if there was anything to stop them getting married then she'd have to say no and pray that the vicar would see the wisdom of keeping his mouth shut and all. They'd make their vows and she'd wear his ring and have a wonderful trousseau. And she'd go off with him and live happily ever after and no one ever needed to know any different.

This was the way I saw it now anyway and I could only hope and pray that my girlie would be able to see it this way too.

Oh what horrors we all had to endure later that day, to see my nephew all covered in blood and gore. I'll never forget that chilling sight. He was dead at the hands of that young usurper who had wormed his way into my family's celebration and now he had stolen the life of my beloved nephew. He was like a son to me, as dear to me as my own daughter. My brother had entrusted him to me and here was the result thanks to that evil boy and his stupid petty squabbling. The feud between the families had reached new heights. I no longer cared what had been agreed about matters between the families. This was our tragedy and it demanded revenge. I demanded it.

They say revenge is sweet. But I was filled with such a bitter thirst for it, that I couldn't imagine any sweetness in its realisation. I wanted him dead and I'm not ashamed to admit that. Why should he continue to live and breathe when my nephew was lying cold and dead? Why should he be able to gloat at our misfortune when we were condemned to mourn forever? Yes, we were condemned by his callous action.

And what was it all over? It was so petty. He had done wrong by showing up here uninvited to take advantage of our magnanimity and to revel in my nephew's humiliation. I knew he was laughing at him. This had nothing to do with honour, with higher feelings, with principles or with values. It was sheer wanton one-upmanship. What kind of motive is that to take the life of a noble and upright young man?

When I saw the body, my breath was all sucked out of me. What revulsion I felt, what horror encompassed me! The shock and the sheer dreadfulness of the sight of him was like a physical blow to my stomach. It took all my breath away and I couldn't speak, only wail my misery. And hovering over all the wretchedness was my own guilt. It was my fault. I had goaded him. I had encouraged him to teach the boy a lesson. It was I who said he would get what was coming to him. And now I felt that all over again, only this time what was coming to him was much worse. He deserved to suffer for the suffering he had inflicted on us. I had to keep telling myself that I was not responsible. It was he who was responsible and he must be made to pay for it, to pay the price of his heartless disrespect for all that is important and correct. Right there on the paving stones of the town square, splattered with my family's blood, I demanded revenge.

One of the boy's family members was there as a witness to what had happened. He sought to blame the whole thing on my nephew, saying that it was he who had started it, although he did not hesitate to name the perpetrator. He tried to make out that the boy had spoken gently and had not wanted to fight. He claimed that my nephew had refused to listen to his attempts at keeping the peace. What outrage to speak ill of the dead and to bend the truth to serve his own purposes! He claimed that my nephew had killed one of their friends. How dare he accuse one who cannot defend himself! It was obvious to me that he was lying to make his friend sound better. There must have been a good twenty of them involved in this brawl, but it was my nephew who was lying there dead and the boy who killed him was going to have to pay for it. I demanded justice. The boy's father was there amongst the crowd. He too sought to defend him, saying he was revenging the life of his friend. When I arrived there I tried to catch his eye, but all the man would do was look at the ground. What shame he must have been feeling for his son's foul behaviour. He would not even look me in the eye.

The boy had run away like the coward that he was. He was escaping punishment, but only temporarily. This left me free to plan my own revenge. It wouldn't be sweet, but it would be satisfying and I relished the prospect of it.

Eight

I went to her room in such a state. I was upset about her cousin and I was the one who had to tell her. Of course I was upset. I'd known him since he was just a little mite too. And not only did I have to tell her that he had been killed, but I had to tell her who had done it. What would she think? What would she say? What would she do? The irony of love and hate was so cruel for her to have to bear. Would she even believe it? I just didn't know what to say.

I went over it again and again in my mind: he's dead, he's dead. He's been killed. Oh no, everything's gone wrong … When I came in she asked me if I had the rope. The rope? Oh yes, the rope. I had the rope. He's dead, he's dead. He's been killed. Oh everything's gone wrong … And before I even realised it, I was saying it out loud.

"He's dead! Oh, my girlie, he's dead. Everything's gone wrong."

"What?"

"He's dead. Your young man, he …"

"What? My …? What, he's dead?"

"Your young man …"

"No, it can't be. It can't be. I can't live without him. Stop it. It's not true."

"They brought him back here. I saw the blood. He was all covered in blood and I saw it. I near passed out at the sight of it."

"Oh, my heart will just break. It's all over for me. My life is over."

"Oh, my girlie, your poor cousin … your poor, poor cousin. I can't believe he's dead."

"What?" She looked at me like I was telling her for the first time. "They're *both* dead? My cousin *and* my husband?"

We stared at each other. I stopped dead and I realised that she hadn't understood what I was telling her.

"No, my girlie. It's your husband who killed your cousin and now he's going to have to get away from here, get away from here and stay away for ever."

She was silent for a moment, taking it in. Slowly she repeated it. "It's my husband who killed my cousin? He did it?" I nodded slowly.

"He destroyed part of my family? How could he? How could he do that to me?" She buried her face in her hands and wailed. "Is he some kind of monster or is he the gentle person I love? How can I love someone so hateful? Is he a saint or is he a devil? How could someone so wonderful do something so vile?" She was all confusion and disbelief.

"Ah, that's men for you," I said. "What man can you trust? They're all rats. Shame on him," I said. "Shame on that boy."

Suddenly she turned on me.

"How dare you," she raged. "How dare you say that!"

"Girlie, he killed your cousin. How could you say anything else about him?"

"And how could I say anything bad about my husband?" My, she was confused. Blowing hot and cold, changing every moment with the torment of it. She ran the fingers of both hands through her hair and sobbed, looking at me, but seeing nothing.

"How could you do it?" I took a breath, but then realised she wasn't talking to me. "How could you kill my cousin when we've only been married three hours? Was it self defence? Would he have killed you? Then I'd have my cousin, but would have lost my husband. So he died and I still have you." She tried to work through it as if there was some sort of logic that could make it make sense. "So he's dead and you have to leave." And she hung her head in despair. "Losing you is worse than any death." That sounded so dramatic, but then it *was* dramatic. It was life and death.

I waited, so as not to intrude on her grief. Finally I spoke.

"Girlie." She was silent. "Girlie," I said. "I think I know where he'll be hiding. I'll bring him to you. You *will* have your night with him."

"Yes, go and find him," she sniffed. "It will be our farewell." And she pulled her ring off her finger. "Here," she said flatly. "Give him this. Then he'll know I want him to come." I wiped the sweat off my hand and took it from her, placing it carefully into my pocket.

As we returned home I was full of the wretchedness of my loss. My husband had said nothing. He was silent and brooding, almost like an adolescent himself. I needed to know what he was thinking. Did he think like me? Why had he said nothing? I wanted him to step up and defend my family, be manly and demand the justice we deserved. It should not be left to me to speak up for what was right. He was the man of the family, the head of the family. He should speak out. He should act.

We came back to the house with my nephew's body and all was in turmoil. The whole household was in uproar with weeping and moaning and cries for revenge. And all this time my husband remained taciturn, whereas I needed to give voice to my thoughts. I found myself begging him to speak. I needed to hear that he shared my opinion, that he shared my desire for retribution.

"Why are you so silent?" I beseeched. "Why do you not cry out in anger?"

"This is my way," he replied steadily. "I am not one for extravagant displays of emotion. You know that."

"Yes," I found myself almost whispering, as if I were a poorly behaved child asking for something that was unreasonable. Suddenly the feeling got the better of me and I began to sob. I sobbed for my nephew and I sobbed for myself. I felt the loss so keenly. I had been channelling my emotions into thoughts of revenge, but now I just gave way to my sorrow. How could a young life be completely extinguished so quickly? How could I ever recover from the loss and how could I ever forgive myself for having egged him on? The waves of wretched weeping consumed my whole being and I fell against my husband for comfort. I leaned on his sturdy shoulder and let out

my howls of grief. His arms gradually enfolded me and I relied on his strength to hold me up as the pain was wrung out of me in my cries.

"All will be well," he said. "We will have our revenge. We are proud and we will prevail by rising above their sordid deeds. That boy is nothing. He can't run away from what he has done. He has sinned against all that is right and we will have our revenge." His voice was low and steady and I was comforted by it. I looked up into his eyes and saw there what I loved about him. There were tears brimming on his eyelids, but I knew not to draw attention to his emotion. He was a proud man who dismissed tearful demonstrations as a sign of unmanly weakness. Nevertheless I loved him for it and knew that we were allies in our mourning and in our hunger for vengeance. No more words were necessary. I just leaned against him and took strength from him.

After a while a new thought came to me. What of our daughter? What of her happiness? Where had all our triumph of the previous day melted away to? I voiced my thoughts quietly to my husband.

"What about our daughter?" I asked. "What about her marriage?"

"Shhh," he responded. "Don't you worry about that. I'll take care of everything. I'll see to everything. Everything will be all right."

I nestled into his shoulder in the knowledge that his strength of character would bring us through this. Of course he would take care of everything. He always did. And despite my sorrow, I felt a kind of hope kindling inside me. I leaned against him, grateful for his warmth and his strength.

Nine

I went out into the warm summer night and headed out along the road that would take me to the miserable little vicarage. That must be where he was hiding. Where else would he be? Who else would give him the time of day? It was just getting dark and I could smell the sweet smell of evening flowers. I think it was honeysuckle. I can't smell that smell now without thinking of that night. It reminds me of my girlie's sadness. It's a sad smell to me. Can smells be sad? Well, they can to me.

So here I was, on yet another errand. What a day this had been! Was it really only twenty-four hours earlier that I had been all excitement that my girlie was to meet her future husband? My mind was reeling. What were my girlie's options now? One thing was clear to me. She had no future with this boy, married or not, it made no difference. How could I persuade her to carry on with her life without him? As if this had never happened? That was what she had to do. Time is a great healer, but what does a young person in love know about time and its ability to dull the pain that she was feeling right now? Would I even be able to persuade her to keep the events of today a secret? I would certainly be willing to keep *my* mouth shut at that point in the wedding service when the vicar says does anyone know of any impediment to the marriage? It certainly wouldn't be an impediment as far as I am concerned. I'd be all the more eager for her to marry someone else and get this out of her system forever.

I knew my way, even in the dark and although it couldn't have taken me long to get there, it felt like an eternity. I just wanted everything to be over and my girlie to start getting over it. As I approached the dingy vicarage I could see a candle burning through the open window. As I stood nearby I could hear them talking. It was him all right.

"What am I going to do?" he was wailing. "Tell me what to do." I'd tell him what to do all right. Just do us all a favour and take your sorry rear end out of our lives for good.

"You must leave, my son," is what he told him. "You'll escape with your life as long as you're never seen here again."

"Huh!" he said. "I'd be better off dead if I have to slink off and disappear off the face of the earth." He spat out the words with disdain. There was still something cocky in his tone and I felt even more than ever that I had been right about him. "I might just as well be dead. Dead? Outlawed? What's the difference? There's nowhere else worth living. You might as well just cut my head off." Why didn't these thoughts occur to him *before* he let his anger get the better of him?

"It's a sin to speak that way," said the vicar. Why, oh lordy was he wasting his time on him? "It's a mercy that you have the chance to get away. Open your eyes, my son." He spoke harshly enough, but his words were indulgent. That's the trouble with the clergy. They see the good in everyone.

"You call that a mercy?" said the boy. "I call it a living hell. Being here with her is paradise. Everything else is hell."

Then go to hell is what I thought to myself. Excuse my language, but he was just behaving like the spoilt brat that he was. What the hell did she see in him?

"Why can't I be with her?" he yelled. "I'm the one who needs to be with her and I'm the one who can't. You say that's not torture? You say I'll be better off? You say that's better than death?" He stamped his foot and slammed his fist into the wall with such force, it near on made me jump right out of my skin.

There was that temper again. It was a flash of viciousness; nasty, cruel and violent. Oh, my girlie, I wish you would see you'd be better off without him. I wish you could see him through my old eyes. I like to think there's enough wisdom in them to see things the way they really are. Right now that boy looked absolutely pathetic. I'm afraid that's all I can say. He was just a pathetic little boy in a strop. What's so attractive about that, I ask you? Tell me that.

"Just listen to me," pleaded the vicar, so gently that I wanted to stick my head through that window and say you do as you're told, you snivelling little maggot, or I'll put you across my knee if he's not going to teach you the lesson you deserve. I may be a weak and feeble woman, but I wouldn't put up with that sort of talk. Mind you, I had never put my girlie across my knee. There was no need for that sort of thing. All she needed was a little guidance and she knew how to do the right thing. She had her own little conscience way back when she was a tiny little mite. But this lad was a different kettle of fish altogether. Love is blind *and* deaf and stupid too, if you ask me.

"Just listen," said the vicar again. "We'll work something out. You've got to be strong."

Him, be strong? I shook my head and tutted to myself. This vicar chappy wouldn't know a lost cause if it bit him in the arse. Why was he wasting his breath? That boy thought being strong meant throwing his weight about and getting one over on someone else. He thought it meant getting your revenge and coming out on top, whatever the cost.

"You call running away being strong? I'm not interested in your philosophy. It can't change anything. It can't bring her to me. It can't do anything, so you can just shove it." He was shrieking like a maniac.

"You're not listening to me."

"Can't you see? You don't know how I feel. If you were young and in love like me, then you'd understand. In love. Newly married. A murderer. An outlaw. If you only knew how I felt ..."

I didn't want to hear any more, so I knocked quietly on the door. The vicar heard the knocking and told him to go and hide, but he wouldn't. I knocked again.

"Who's there?" I heard the vicar say.

In answer I knocked again and I heard him scuffling around in there in a right panic. I knocked once more and I heard the vicar again.

"Who is it? What do you want?"

"Let me in for gawd's sake and I'll tell you," I answered. "I've come on an errand from this young man's bride." He opened the door finally and I just about tumbled into the tiny room.

"So where is he then?" I asked. The vicar pointed downwards and he was lying there on the floor blubbering like a baby.

"My goodness," I said. "She's in just the same state, snivelling and whimpering all over the place. Come on, get up," I said, giving him a little shove with my toe. "It's pathetic. Get up and be a man."

He blubbered something I couldn't understand.

"Oh my, what a pretty mess," I said to him. "What a pretty mess indeed."

"How is she? What did she say? Have I spoilt everything? Does she just think I'm a murderer?"

"Oh, she hasn't said much at all. Just weeping and crying and moaning and howling. She's crying over him and she's crying over you."

"Oh, I've ruined everything and I hate myself. There's nothing left to live for." And he pulled out a knife. It made me jump I can tell you and it scared me half to death to see him waving it around wildly like he was.

"Now pull yourself together," said the vicar. "Be a man. Stop those girlish tears and let's have no more of that nonsense. You should be ashamed of yourself for talking that way. I don't want to hear any more about you doing away with yourself, do you hear me? That would be the death of her too. You are letting everybody down. Get a grip." The boy just stood there and the vicar finally let him have it.

"Stop wallowing in what you've lost. You're lucky you're not the one who's dead. Look at what you have. You still have a beautiful new wife. What about what *she* needs? Go to her. Go spend some time with her before you have to leave. We'll find a way to make things right. When everything has blown over we'll be able to tell the secret of your marriage and find a way to get you a pardon. Look to the future."

Woh, bless my soul. It would seem he was no fool after all, that vicar. The lad finally got the message. He looked down in despair, hanging his head in acquiescence. He was going to do what he was told for once. We hastily made our plans. It was my job to go home and make sure that everyone in the house was asleep. I would tell her he was coming. Then he would come to her as planned and stay until dawn when he'd have to make his getaway. I wouldn't want to imagine what would happen if he got caught there. But it was worth the risk to give them the chance to say goodbye. As far as I was concerned if she never saw him again it would be too soon, but saying their farewells would help her accept it ... I hoped. I wasn't interested in saving his skin, only in helping her get over it.

I thrust my hand into my pocket. And then I remembered the ring. I pulled it out and held it up.

"She said to give you this." You should have seen his eyes light up as he grabbed it. This meant that she wanted to see him, that she could forgive him. I told him he'd better get a move on. I said my goodbyes to the well-meaning clergyman and rushed back to tell her the news.

My husband did take action that very evening. We met with the hopeful young suitor who so earnestly desired to please my daughter. He came to the house to express his condolences and to ask after the poor girl's tender heart.

My husband told him that the girl was very attached to her cousin. She was shut away in her room mourning and probably needed to get a good night's rest. The young man responded so graciously. He said he realised that now was not the time to be pressing his suit. He said his goodnights and asked me to give her his best wishes. I felt great affection for him and tremendous gratitude for his kindly attitude. I assured him that I would speak to her of him the next morning. She was far too distressed to be approached that night.

My husband however was unwilling to let him go without an answer. He told him that he believed that she would be guided by her father on such matters. In fact he was quite sure of it. He suggested that before I go to bed I go to see her and tell her that he had decided on the matter. His plan was that she was to be married on Wednesday. This was quite a shock. It was already Monday. That gave hardly any time to make the arrangements. Well in that case it would be Thursday. And so it was decided. On Thursday she would be married and he would be glad to call the young man "son". It was soon, but considering the circumstances of the loss of our nephew we would make it a simple affair with just a few friends present.

The young man was so excited at the prospect, he could hardly believe his luck. He said he wished that Thursday was tomorrow! And so our business was concluded. I was to go to see our daughter to prepare her for what was planned. I wasn't altogether sure of how she would react right now. Only this morning she had seemed so thrilled at the idea and I had been busy hurrying things along with her father. But now? How things can change in the blink of an eye. I had no idea of how she would react now to have the whole business concluded so quickly. Perhaps it would console her, but perhaps she would be saddened not to have the joyful wedding celebration that we had always dreamed of for her. I wondered if she would find it distasteful to think of such things on the day of her cousin's death.

So I decided against going to her that night. I would leave her to her own grief and would talk to her in the morning when, with the benefit of a good night's sleep, she would be more likely to look favourably on what her father had decided for her. Yes, no doubt that was best. In the morning I would approach her in the light of a new day and she would be able to think of the future.

It was however a long time before I went to bed that night. My mind was reeling with the pace of events during those two short days. I forced myself to think positively, to think about the joy I had seen in her face that morning and how sure I was that she would want to marry the man we had chosen for her. I had promised her to speak to her father, to move things along for her, to make her joy complete. But now I was doubting her reaction. The shock of today's events would have taken its toll. She was a sensitive girl and prone to the mood swings so common in girls of her age. I would have to remain positive and she would follow my lead. Her father wished to console her for her loss. This would give her something wonderful to look forward to. What better consolation to heal her broken heart? We would bury her cousin, then we would rejoice in all the good and beautiful things in life by celebrating her marriage to this fine young man. The future would compensate for the past. I too would find great comfort in this.

Ten

What a night that was! I didn't get a wink of sleep sitting watch outside that door and by the sound of things, I'm sure they didn't get any sleep either, if you follow me. I tried not to listen, but you can imagine what it was like. I had to keep alert to listen for footsteps on the stairs and it's no mean feat to keep one ear open and the other closed, I can tell you. I heard their muffled voices and their stifled sighs and it was almost as if I could feel their hot breath. Could I really hear the rustle of the bedclothes or was it just my mind working overtime? No, I shouldn't have been listening, but wait a minute, was that a sound on the stairs? Shhhh! Now it was so dead quiet I could hear their whispers of love. Was I just imagining that I could hear their moist kisses? It gave my own heart a flutter. I felt like whistling or humming, so that all I could hear would be my own noise. But then I would drown out the sound of those footsteps on the stairs that I so feared to hear. Just the thought of those footsteps kept me silent and awake. And so the night went on.

And as I sat there my thoughts went round and round. I felt guilty. Yes, I felt guilty all right. I've always thought that guilt was almost always misplaced. After all, you can only feel guilty if you've done something you thought was wrong and if you thought it was wrong, you wouldn't have done it in the first place, would you? You always do the best you can with the information you have at the time. There's never anything to feel guilty about. But then why was I feeling so guilty right now? Was it more a matter of regret that if I'd known then what I know now, I would have done something different? Perhaps I felt guilty because I already did know, in a way, what I know now. I knew he was no good. I knew he was a smooth-talking so-and-so who probably didn't mean a word of it. I knew he had already been bonkers over some other girl and *that* didn't last. I already didn't trust him any further than I could throw him.

But I didn't stop her. There were things I could have done to get in the way. I could have dragged her in off that balcony before she'd pledged her troth. I could have conveniently just not found him when I went out looking for him. I could have told him she wasn't interested. I could have told her *he* wasn't interested. (Although she would have known I was lying. I'm a terrible liar). I could have done lots of things differently. I didn't stop her.

More than guilty though, I just felt terribly sad for her. She was so full of joy only yesterday and now she was in the depths of despair. I couldn't stand to see my girlie like that. How would she be tomorrow? How would she cope with losing him? How could I help her then? It hurts so much to see your child suffer. All her life I have tried to protect her, then overnight events take hold and all of a sudden there's nothing you can do. My reason was telling me she would just have to get over it, to do what her parents wanted, to forget any of this ever happened. But was she ever going to be able to forget this even if she wanted to? What a bloody awful mess.

And so I sat there, minute after minute, hour after hour, wallowing in my own thoughts. When dawn was finally breaking and I could hear stirrings in other parts of the house, I thought it wasn't safe to leave them alone any longer. I started banging about and bustled into the room, trying to keep my eyes firmly on the floor. I couldn't help but notice they were still firmly locked in each other's arms. Oh, the joys of young love!

"It's time for you two to get a move on," I said. "We are not the only ones in the house who are awake. Her ladyship is up and I'm sure she's on her way up here. It's time for young Mr. Smartypants to hop it out the window." I went out of the door, but left it open to make sure they really were saying goodbye. I was surprised to hear him asking for just one kiss as he climbed out. She was calling him her lover, her man, her best friend and asking him to keep in touch with her every day.

"Will we ever see each other again?" she called leaning down towards him.

He rushed away, promising to be true to her. It was not a moment later that I heard her ladyship's footsteps on the stairs and in she waltzed. Lord love us, I'm glad he was gone because I don't think my poor nerves could stand much more of this. It certainly was odd for her to come to my girlie's room so early in the morning, but these were odd times indeed.

"Well, my girl," said the lady, "How are you feeling?"

"Not well at all."

"Still crying over the death of your poor cousin? I know it was a great shock, but come, come, it's time to dry your tears. I know you were very close and it's good to let out your feelings, but too much crying really isn't good for you. Crying is not going to bring him back."

"Just let me cry. I've suffered such a loss." She glanced up at me through her lowered eyelashes. *I* knew what she meant. She meant she'd lost her lover, not her cousin. Not that she didn't feel that loss, but she was too wrapped up in her romance to feel much of anything else right now and it was just as well that her ladyship had made her assumptions and was not really paying much attention anyway. It seemed to me she was more angry than distressed about her nephew. It looked like, in my humble opinion, it was just more fuel for the fire of hatred between the families as far as she was concerned.

"That evil murderer has got away," said her ladyship, "but don't you fret. We'll have our revenge against him, don't you fear. I'm going to send someone to find him where he's hiding and give him a taste of his own medicine. Don't you worry, my girl. I'm going to have him put to sleep permanently." Oh my, how shocking is the thirst for revenge. I looked at my girlie to see her reaction. She barely trembled as she replied, "Anyone who would hurt someone so close to me would deserve all he got." Well, I knew who she was thinking of, but her ladyship was completely unsuspecting. Why would she mean anything other than what she heard her saying—that she too wanted to revenge the death of her cousin? Our eyes met and she lowered them quickly, afraid that she would give herself away and let out her true feelings for that boy. Her secret was safe with me. I was glad it was over and he was gone. It was time for her to let things rest, to let time pass and do what her parents asked, if not in her heart, then at least in appearances for the time being. Time can heal many things and for the very young, what seems to go in a flash for old fogeys like me, could seem half an eternity. She would get over it in time, with my help.

"Yes," said her ladyship, "we'll take care of that and you can rest easy. But that's enough of that. I came to bring you some good news."

"How could there be any good news at a time like this?" said my girlie.

"There will be, there will be. Your father has decided that you need something to take away all this misery. You need something joyful to set your mind on." She smiled broadly and took my girlie's hand. I have to say that my thoughts matched my girlie's—this was just not the moment.

Her ladyship continued, "Your father has decided to turn this Thursday into a wonderful joyful day by making it your wedding day. He has spoken to that wonderful young man and has arranged everything. Thursday it is!"

My girlie's eyes widened in horror as she pulled her hand away. "No! I can't, I won't marry him. It's too soon. I couldn't possibly. I'm not going to do it and you can tell that to my father. Why, I'd rather marry that evil murderer!" Oh yes, she's a clever one, my girlie.

"Well, you can tell that to your father yourself then, my girl. He'll be up here in a minute." And he was—there were the dreaded footsteps on the stairs yet again. I looked from my girlie to her ladyship to the open door. The three of us stood frozen, waiting for the master to show his face. How would he react, what would he say when he heard my girlie's wilful refusal? He strode in, all indulgence and smiles and looked down at my girlie's downcast face. He saw the tears flashing wet on her cheeks.

"Well, well, well," he began kindly. "Still crying? It's like a flood here with all these tears." He cupped her chin with his hand, but she wouldn't raise her eyes to him. He looked at his wife. "Have you told her what we've decided?"

"Oh yes, I've told her, but she wants nothing to do with it."

"Nothing to do with it? What sort of talk is that? No, no, I can't believe that. Isn't she grateful that we would choose such an excellent match for her? Wouldn't she be proud to be the wife of such a rich and generous man?"

His question was addressed to his wife, but it was my girlie who answered him, bold as brass, pouting that lower lip, just like she did when she was a little girl. "Yes, I'm grateful that you would want to do that for me, but I can't be proud to marry someone you have chosen. The whole idea is hateful to me."

"What? Well, my girl, proud or not, hateful or not, you'll do as you're told and marry the man if I have to drag you there myself." And he began ranting and railing at her like you wouldn't believe. All about how she was their only child and they thought she was a blessing, but she turned out to be a curse and they should never have had her. He wouldn't let her have her say. She begged him to listen to her, but he wouldn't have any of it. He told her she'd be at that church or he'd disown her forever. I couldn't stand to hear it and I tried to intervene.

"She's a real blessing, sir," I said. "You shouldn't treat her that way." I think he was surprised to hear me speak up.

"You'll mind your own business," he spluttered, giving me the eyeballs of death. "Just who do you think you are?"

"I'm only telling the truth," I threw back, but he didn't like that one bit.

"Shut up, you blithering idiot," he yelled. "I'm not interested in what you have to say."

His poor wife tried to get him to cool down a bit, but there was no holding him back. Ranting away, he was. It was like a hurricane of fury. On and on he went about how he'd only ever planned to make her a good match, to find her a fine gentleman and all the care he'd taken to do that for her, only for her to throw it all back in his face. He was spitting it all out in a rage. Said it was tommy rot that she wasn't ready, that she was too young. It wasn't up to her to say when she was ready to wed. He had made his mind up and he wasn't going back on his word. Thursday it would be and she'd better think about it or he'd throw her out. And with that he stormed out, slamming the door behind him. Well, I never!

My girlie ran to her ladyship and begged her to take her side, just to let her have a little time. It was too soon, she couldn't get married now. But the lady wasn't going to budge. She obviously felt like she couldn't go against her husband. She set her face in a firm grimace and walked out, refusing to do a thing.

Now there were just the two of us. She ran to me and took both my hands, holding them together like she was praying and wanted me to pray with her.

"What shall I do?" she pleaded. "What shall I do? Tell me what to do. I already have a husband. I can't get married. It's a sin. What should I do? Help me, help me, help me. Say something that will make me feel better."

I wish there had been something that I could have said that would have helped. I had tried to defend her to the master, but he wasn't going to listen. His mind was made up and now we were facing a problem that had no real solution. I already wished I had never gone along with it all in the first place. What a pretty mess. What a pretty mess indeed. Well, I had said it would come to no good and I wasn't impressed with anything that boy had said or done. He was so fickle. One minute he was in love with that other girl and the next minute it was my girlie. He was just living for the moment and now he was gone, leaving her to cry. And why hadn't he just walked away? Why did he have to fight? It was all passion and revenge with him. Would it really have been my girlie's cousin or him? Did he have to kill him to defend himself? That's what she believes, but it doesn't make much sense to me. I can understand her ladyship's anger against that boy, not that I share her idea of a solution. She too only wants revenge and what good does that do? They say revenge is sweet. No, it's not. It's bitter, bitter, bitter. And it's cruel. It just leads to more pain. Walking away is the strong thing to do. That's the way to teach someone a lesson. *I* was angry with that boy and all. But for what he did to my girlie, not her poor cousin. He was gone and she was left to pick up the pieces of her life.

I had to tell her what I thought. She was asking for some comfort from me, but sometimes you just have to swallow the bitter medicine. I remember when I was a child and I was ill, my mother used to stroke my hair and say she wished she could have my illness for me. I thought that was such a strange thing to say. Why would anyone want to be ill? But of course when I became a mother I understood and I would stroke my girlie's hair and tell her I wished I could have her pain. That's how I felt now. I have suffered all the joy and the pain that young love has to offer and come out the other side stronger and better for it. If only I could suffer it for her now.

I took a deep breath. I knew that this wasn't what she wanted to hear. "Well, this is the way I see it." I paused, hesitating. I wasn't expecting her to react well, but I wanted her to know I was on her side.

"Your new husband is gone," I went on, "And he's not coming back. He can't. So you might as well accept that and carry on with your life." I kept talking. Could she read the concern and the love behind my words? "Marry the man who's been chosen for you. He's a fine man and a good man. That boy's not worthy to lick his boots. This second husband will be much better for you than the first. That's what I say." And I nodded my head emphatically. That was it. That was what I thought. Yes, that was the way I looked at it, but she turned away from me and somehow I couldn't look her in the eye. She was right. It was a sin. I was telling her to take the easy path and just pretend nothing had ever happened. I suppose it wasn't really the easy path as far as she was concerned. I suppose there wasn't an easy path.

She sat there quietly. She just looked down. She couldn't meet my eyes any more than I could meet hers. I could hear her breathing. It seemed like the tears were going to come again.

"Is that what you really think?" she said, twisting the material of her nightgown in her fingers.

"Yes, my girlie. That's what I think."

"Thank you."

"What do you mean, girlie?"

"Thank you," she repeated. "I feel better now." She continued to twist the material. "I think I'll go and talk to the vicar."

"Yes. That's a good idea," I said.

I should have known that we were no longer on the same path. I should have realised that she was shutting me out right there and then. I should have heard it in her tone. I should have felt it in the air. But I was too busy telling myself that everything was going to turn out all right. Too busy pretending. I didn't want to notice that she was avoiding my eyes as she got dressed in silence. I didn't want to notice the invisible wall she was silently building between us. Perhaps in a way I did know, but I had said my piece. I had taken a position and it wasn't on the same side of the fence she wanted to be. Now she was making her plans without me. And off she went to confide in someone else. It felt like I was losing her right at that moment.

Despite my misgivings and my decision to wait until the morning, I was unprepared for the intensity of her reaction. She had always been a strong-willed child and I blamed the nurse for indulging her way too much. But I never imagined that she would wilfully disobey her parents in this way. I had hoped she would be grateful and although I thought she might not be enthusiastic to get married so soon after the loss of her cousin, I never expected an outright refusal.

When she had looked at me with such a pleading expression I wanted to tell her that I understood, that it was natural that she should feel like this at such a time. My mother's heart was telling me to give her a little time. She would come round if we just gave her time. I thought of her happiness the morning before. Of course she would come round in time. But I couldn't go against my husband. It was time that we didn't have. He had made his decision and he had given his word. He couldn't go back on it and I had to support him, publicly at least. How I envied the nurse that she could stand up for the girl when I could not. It was she who was telling him that the girl was a blessing. She was the one who seemed to understand her heart and I was left to appear heartless and cold. My heart ached, but there was nothing I could do.

When I left my daughter and the nurse alone I felt cold and empty. I admit that I had felt jealous that she could be the kind and motherly one while I had to remain stern. I felt like she had robbed me of my rightful relationship with my daughter and all because she didn't have a relationship with her father. She didn't have any duty, except to be loving and affectionate to my daughter. It was unfair and it left me feeling all the more bereft and powerless.

I resolved at least to speak to my husband. What harm was there in that? I went to his study and knocked gently.

"Come in," he bellowed. I was right. I knew that I would find him there. When I entered timidly I found him stomping around with a harsh expression on his face.

"What do you want?" he growled. Again I was right. There was going to be no changing his mind. That much was clear.

I sighed and shook my head.

"I wondered if there was anything I could do for you" I ventured, not wanting to rile him any more.

"What is there that could be done?" he roared. "What could turn that ungrateful girl into the obedient daughter I expected her to be?"

"She will come around," I said simply. "She will realise what you are doing for her and she will be grateful."

"You're darn right she will," he spluttered, the spit flying. "She will if she knows what's good for her!" He was pacing around.

"*I* will *keep my word*," he went on. "She shall *obey me and she shall marry him as arranged.* There's an end to it and I'll have no one say any different."

"*Of course*," I said. "*You know what's best and she'll realise that in time. She won't refuse you, not when it really comes down to it. I'll talk to her again.*"

"*What's the point of talking to her if she's just going to be wilful and rebellious? Tell me that.*"

"*I'll talk to her when she has cooled down a little. She'll see sense. She knows you only ever have her best interests at heart.*"

I put my hands on his shoulders and gently massaged them. He was so tense.

"*Just relax,*" I said. "*She'll come around.*"

And gradually I felt the tension relaxing from his shoulders. He was a proud man and he would never go back on his word. We both knew that. I just hoped it would end well for all of us.

Eleven

When she came back from her visit to the vicar she was tight-lipped and distant. Still she avoided my eyes and there was a cool and weighty silence between us. I knew that there was much to tell despite her silence. I knew that things were not the way she would tell them to the world and yet I wasn't able to voice those thoughts. Suddenly I too was part of that outside world to her. I knew it, but I couldn't say so. It was too painful.

She told his lordship that she had been to talk to the clergyman and that she would no longer be disobedient to him. She would do whatever he wanted. All the time she avoided my eyes. This was what I had advised her to say, but it didn't ring true to me at all. I knew she had no intention of doing what he wanted. The master jumped on it though, as if to hesitate would make her change her mind again. Did he too know instinctively that she was planning something else? Were we all just going through the motions? He wanted to send for her intended right away and tell him that the wedding was to be the next day instead of Thursday. Her ladyship seemed to think that this was unnecessarily rushing things, but her husband was insistent. My girlie asked me to come and help her get herself ready. This wasn't the joy with which I had always imagined we would conspire together to prepare for her wedding, but I went with her, unable to find the words to ask her what she was really planning to do tomorrow. She said nothing and continued to look down. I felt like she was punishing me for my unwillingness to see things her way. But I just didn't see that she had any realistic options.

We walked to her room in silence. I searched for a way to break the silence, but it was too heavy on me, pressing down on me. In that dreadful quiet I felt alone with my worst fears. I feared that there would be no tomorrow for her, that she would never wake on that day that was supposed to be the beginning of her new life. But how could these fears find voice? I was desperate, but there was nothing I could do. She had shut me out and that was the end of it.

Back in the room I hoped that she might open up to me, but it was not to be. I began to busy myself with her clothes for the next day. She showed no interest. Instead she brushed my arm with the briefest touch of her fingertips.

"Those clothes are fine," she said. Her tone was dry and flat. "They'll do fine. Now just leave me alone. I want to be alone with my conscience tonight. You know what a heavy heart I have." Yes, I did know. Why could I not talk to her? Why could I not tell her what was in *my* heart?

I didn't know what to say. My head was telling me I was saying goodbye to her for the last time. My heart didn't want to hear it. I was already grieving for the loss of her. How could I find a way to make that simple word, "goodbye" contain all that I wanted to say to her? No words would have been enough. I needed one more moment alone with her, but it was not to be. There was a tap on the door and in came the mistress. She thought it was her place to be there that night. She came to offer her help, but my girlie said that she didn't need any help. She said that we should go together and leave her alone. I felt the cruelty of her words. She didn't want me any more than she wanted the woman who had given her life, but had never given her love. She sent us both away with the same gesture. I tried to linger at the door for one more moment with her. Her ladyship went out of the room and I hesitated, so that for a brief moment our eyes met and my look said to her what my words could not.

Her ladyship and I were to busy ourselves with details of the cooking for the next day, although I knew there was to be no feast. The master was in a fine mood. He was an ostrich with his head in the sand and couldn't be persuaded to go to bed. We would be up all night with the preparations for an event that was never to be. There would be all kinds of bustle, what with carrying things to and from the kitchen. The servant boys would be up and down the stairs, whinging and whining like you wouldn't believe. All I would be able to do would be to sigh and think about my lovely girlie. As I turned and shut the door behind me I whispered, "My love is always with you," but she didn't hear me.

When my daughter came back from talking with the clergyman there was a huge change in her demeanour and it made me uneasy. Instead of wilful and defiant she was sullen, yet compliant. I wondered what the fellow must have said to her to bring about this change and it was so extreme that I felt anxious. I tried to push those thoughts away. After all, this was the change that we had desired. We would be able to marry her as we had planned. There was no pleasure however in the transformation. She was not happy, just expressionless and empty. It was as if the fight had been knocked out of her. She had given in. I consoled myself with the thought that time would heal her loss and that as she grew to know her husband, she would grow to love him indeed. The feelings that she had displayed the morning after she met him would return. The excitement would come back. Perhaps this was what the vicar had told her. Her new love would heal the pain that she was suffering. In time.

My husband's mood had changed too. He was all joviality and conviviality once more, all ready to play host to this happy event and fussing with the cooks and servants. When our daughter returned from her conference he was there to greet her.

"Well, now, my headstrong girl," he said looking at her sideways. "What have you been up to?"

She responded meekly with her eyes on the ground, "I've been to talk things over and think about what I should do. The vicar advised me to tell you that I am sorry for having disobeyed you and from now on I'll do as you ask."

He was thrilled to hear this. All his cheerfulness was restored and he patted her affectionately on the shoulder. My own reaction was somewhat sus-

picious. I looked at the nurse and I could see that she too was anxious. Perhaps it was our woman's intuition.

My husband was all the more eager to have the marriage concluded immediately.

"Let's send for that lucky young man," he said. "Let's tie the knot straight away. No need to wait until Thursday. Tomorrow will be the day."

"I saw him with the vicar," the girl informed us. "He was there. I showed him all the love I could, within the bounds of modesty." She showed no emotion, but this did not deter my husband.

"Well, that's marvellous," he cried. "Good for the vicar. We're all indebted to him."

The girl looked to the nurse to help her prepare her clothes for the next day. I felt a pang of jealousy. Was this not a mother's job? What had I done that I was so cut out of these special moments in her life. She was my only child. Why should I not be the one to share her confidences? I glanced at the nurse. How dare she usurp me in this manner!

"It doesn't have to be tomorrow," I said quickly. I wanted to intervene in some way to establish my right to be involved, but my husband cut me off.

"Nonsense," he smiled. "Go with her now nurse. It'll be your job to get her to the church on time tomorrow morning." I felt bereft and could only watch as my daughter went to prepare for her wedding with the help of another woman instead of me. It was a cruel blow.

After they had gone I looked at my husband.

"We won't have enough food," I said. "Tomorrow is too soon." It was a vain attempt to establish my part in the proceedings.

"Don't worry, don't worry, my dear," said my husband, patting my hand indulgently. "I'll take care of all those details. I shan't be going to bed for a while. Let me be the housewife for once! You go and see to the girl. I'll go and see her happy groom to give him the good news. I'm so happy to see this turn around in the girl."

And off he went to busy himself with all the arrangements. I felt all alone. I made my way to her room, so that I could claim my right to help her prepare for her wedding day.

I tapped on the door and went in without waiting for an answer. It was my right. I smiled, but I could feel the tension already in the room.

"I'm here to help," I said, putting aside my doubts. "There's so much to do."

"No," said my daughter flatly. "We've already got everything ready. I just want to be left alone tonight. You two go and busy yourselves. You must have your hands full with this rush to make the arrangements."

I didn't know what to say. What could I say? If I had felt distant from her in the past, now was not going to be the time to change that. I looked at the nurse. She looked panicked. I said goodnight. What else could I do? I told my daughter to get a good night's sleep. She surely needed it. I looked at the nurse again. She was hesitating, lingering for just a few more moments with her. But she had told both of us to leave her alone. Even the nurse was not going to take my place tonight and I felt a small satisfaction in that. I slipped out quietly, saying no more.

How did I lose my status as her mother? How was I cut out when I had laboured to bring her into the world? I did my duty. I handed her over for the day to day care. I had not meant to hand her over body and soul, but that was how it seemed to be. She was not mine in her heart and I was left with nothing.

Twelve

What happened next was by far the worst thing that can ever happen to a mother. To lose a child is a sorrow beyond imagining. This was the second time it had happened to me, but this was far worse. When I lost my poor newborn lamb, I grieved for all she might have been. I felt cheated that I had nurtured her within me and laboured to give her life, but she was taken from me before I really knew her. I was angry with God. I grieved, but I was consoled by taking my girlie in my arms. But *this* loss … This was a loss without consolation. That morning, the morning that was to be her wedding day, I was sent to wake her. I feared to go into the room, for I knew what I would find. Even so, I still hoped that I had misread her cold signals. She said she was going along with the master and the mistress's wishes. I had told her that was what I thought she should do and she never said that she was thinking otherwise. But I saw the signs. Her coldness towards me was the biggest sign and her quiet acquiescence. She just stopped talking about her life, her love, her plans, her thoughts and feelings. She suddenly put it all away inside her and I was shut out. This time I was angry with myself. It was nothing to do with God. *I* was the parent who had failed her.

I went to the room and I stopped outside the closed door. "Girlie," I called. I closed my eyes and leaned my cheek against the cool wood, my hand on the cold doorknob, cold as death on this summer's morning. The dawn light outside was grey, without a hint of the colour of the season, of the joy of a wedding day. Of course there was no answer. I called again, perhaps not even out loud. I screwed my eyes tight shut as I opened the door. I'm not quite sure exactly what I feared I would see. I even expected the room to smell different. Oh, why had I left her when she asked me to? Left her alone with her desperation, with her misery? This was my sorrow. The regret of letting things lie, blinding myself to what my own senses were telling me. As I cautiously entered the room, I started jabbering to her as if everything was fine and I was waking her on her wedding day. I don't know why I did that. Perhaps I was just trying to make it all right, as if talking to her would make her answer me. I even made rude jokes about how she wouldn't be sleeping like that on her wedding night. But my voice was cracking with terror and woe. I busied myself around the room, gabbling on, as if my jokes would rouse her. But I knew in my heart of hearts that it wasn't going to happen. Finally I came to the bed and dared to look at her. She was still dressed in the same clothes as last night, still and cold on the bed. My sorrow overflowed out of my mouth in the most hideous wail. The mistress was soon in the room, asking what all the noise was about. She saw and she too wailed. We were both too scared to touch her.

I don't know how much time passed, but then the master was in the room, telling us to hurry up for the bridegroom had come for his beautiful bride. I found myself crying out, "She's dead, she's dead, she's dead" through my sobs. My voice was almost not my own. This couldn't be real. I was living in my own nightmare. The master took her in his strong arms but had no voice to speak his misery. He whispered that she was dead, that she was cold, that she was gone. Oh, what horror. It was the worst moment of my life. Worse than losing my dear husband, God rest his soul. No parent should have to live through this. I felt responsible. I was responsible for everything about her. She was my child and she was still just a child. The next few minutes were filled with confusion. The bridegroom came and the vicar came. I couldn't bear to hear the master breathing the words dead and death, over and over. That poor young man had come full of joy and hope only to hear those words. He was inconsolable. Life, love and death can be so cruel. What a woeful, black, hateful day. The vicar was ranting on about heaven and eternal life. Eternal life, my arse. What good was that for us to hear right then? He said she was better off in heaven, but what about us, left here on earth with our guilt and our grief? What good was talk of heaven? What extremes of emotion were running in the house that day. The joy of a wedding had turned to the sorrow of a funeral. The feast was to become a wake. The wedding bouquet would be a wreath.

They were to take her to the family chapel where she was to lie beside her cousin, so recently dead. What a horrible mess all this feuding had caused. And love and marriage did nothing, but make it all ten times worse. My girlie was lost, along with all my dreams of sharing motherhood with her. I was going to tell her about the joys of being the one to nurture and to love. Yes, to love and to cherish, in sickness and in health. This was what love was all about. And now it was all over. All that she held inside her, like a seed waiting to germinate, it was all gone. And all because of him, that boy. Hadn't I said it would come to no good?

A funeral is a strange thing. Sometimes it is not even really sad. It's a kind of celebration of a full life and of all the love the person has experienced in their lifetime. When I lost my own mother it was a little like that. She was a lovely person and many people knew it. We mourned our loss, but the love was still there and we felt comforted by it. It was as if she was there with us, with her comforting arms around us, the way she had always been. But this was a different kind of loss entirely. My girlie was just gone and we were all alone, each with our own silent guilt.

The master's guilt came from the knowledge that he had pushed her too far. He didn't understand her disobedience. After all, he knew best, but he had no idea that this would be the result of his harshness with her. He had thought it was a matter of duty and obedience, even of gratitude for what he was doing for her and for the family. Suddenly he had to realise that it was a matter of the intense feelings of a young girl. It wasn't just defiance, just stubbornness. It was way more than that, but he was now at a loss to understand what it really was at all. To him it was all way out of proportion.

His wife's guilt was for her distance from my girlie. She felt guilty that she had never really been her mother, that she knew nothing about her; that she had never experienced the warmth that comes from holding a child in your arms and looking into her eyes or from hearing her tiny voice telling you she loves you. Perhaps she felt guilty that she hadn't intervened to stop her husband from pushing so hard to get what he wanted from my girlie. She could have begged him to give her more time, but she did nothing. She would just have nothing to do with it. How she must have felt guilty.

Well, what of my thoughts about guilt? What of doing the best thing I could with the situation I was facing and with what I knew at the time? This time there were so many things I might have done differently and I was only left to think what if …? What if I hadn't helped them to be together in secret like that? What if I had spoken up more forcefully when I knew all along it would only end in tears? What if I just hadn't found him for her and made those arrangements? What if I had not left her alone when she silently went to her bed for the last time? Oh, what if …?

And what on earth was the vicar thinking when he was saying all those prayers? What kind of guilt was *he* feeling? Try as I might, I just couldn't catch his eye. As I stood there wallowing in my vat of grief and guilt, I felt my anger bubbling more and more. Yes, I was angry with myself. I had failed my girlie. I had let her down as a mother. But what about him? What had he said to her last night? Why hadn't he saved her when she poured her heart out to him instead of to me? And why would he not meet my gaze now? What was he ashamed of?

I made my decision. I had to talk to him. I had to give him a piece of my mind. He was standing there all holier than thou and I was buggered if I was going to let him get away with it. Ooh, I was simmering mad and he was going to hear about it.

That evening, as the sun was going down, I made my way along the same path that she had followed just the day before. I knew where I was going. As I trod my stomping way, I thought about the last time I had been there, so recently and my anger turned towards that boy. I hoped that *he* was going to feel guilty when he found out what he had done to my girlie. I hoped he was going to feel bloody guilty! He had completely destroyed her and what would he suffer? In a few weeks he'd be on to his next beloved. What a toe-rag! What a heartless cad! He wasn't worth tuppence ha'penny. He got away with it. He got away with it all. He got away with everything he did. He killed her cousin, he had his wicked way with her and now he was off swanning it somewhere while she was lying dead for love of him. And *I* was feeling guilty? I was hopping mad.

When I got there I saw the candle burning in the window, just the same as the other night. Was it only two days ago? I stopped for a moment, just looking at that window. Then I clenched my fists and went stomping up and pounded on the door. I pounded and pounded and I think he must have just about jumped out of his skin.

"Who is it?" came a feeble, hesitating voice.

"Who do you think it is, the Virgin bloody Mary?" I don't know where I found it in me to talk to a vicar that way. I heard scuffling noises inside and he shuffled to the door and opened it just a little to peer out at me. I wasn't going to stand for that and I pushed my way through the door, almost knocking him over as I did so.

"Well?" I sputtered. "Well? What have you got to say for yourself? What did you say to my girlie last night? Why didn't you save her or were you only interested in saving her soul?" He cowered away from me, as I leaned towards him thrusting out my chest and acting as menacing as I could.

"I'm sorry," he almost whispered.

"Sorry?" I said. "Sorry?" I snorted. "Sorry?" I yelled. "I'll give you sorry. You're darn right you're sorry, but what good is that to my poor girlie?"

He looked down and held up his hands, almost like a shrug. "I'm so sorry," was all he could come up with. He still wouldn't look at me. Not properly. He'd just glance at me quickly and look away, as if to make sure he knew what I was doing. "Everything will be all right," he said quietly.

"No it won't," I said. "It'll never be all right."

"No," he said. "No, of course not. I understand what you must be feeling."

"I don't need you to understand," I spat back at him. "It won't help. I just want you to tell me what happened. What did she say? What did you say to her? How did it all go so wrong?" And then, as much to my surprise as to his, I just broke down and sobbed. I wept like a blubbering baby. He put his arms around me and just kept saying, "It will be all right. It will be all right."

When I had got myself back together and sniffed a few times he sat me down with a cup of tea and agreed to tell me what had happened.

"Well, it was a little difficult," he began. "The young man she was supposed to marry came to see me to talk about the arrangements and how her father wanted to speed things up to help her get over the loss of her cousin. I really didn't know what to say. How could I be talking about marrying her to *him,* when I knew she was already married? He was so earnest and I felt so bad for him when she arrived all breathless and was so cold towards him. I don't think he took it badly. He just thought she was being coy with him. She managed to get rid of him by telling him she needed to talk to me alone."

"Yes," I said, "That's what she said to me too." It occurred to me then that she didn't want me to know what she was really thinking any more than she wanted that poor young man to know. I felt so wretched. "But what did she really say to you?" I asked, thinking that he would probably think it was none of my business.

"When he left she urged me to shut the door quickly so she could spill out her heart to me. She was in a right state, saying there was no hope and all was lost. I told her that I knew what had happened and she cried and begged me to find a way to prevent this marriage. She was wild with misery and threatened to kill herself if I didn't do something to stop it."

"And what did you say to her?" I demanded.

He looked down at his hands.

"What *could* I say?" he said. "In a way she was right. There *was* no hope. I ..." he hesitated as though he were ashamed to say it. "I told her to go home and act happy and give her consent to marry the man. I told her it was time to show obedience to her father." He swallowed and kept looking at the floor.

So he had done the same as me. He told her the same as I did. My poor girlie must have felt truly alone. My tears came silently now. We both sat there in the stillness of that dingy little room, both wrapped up in our own thoughts. So God's wisdom was just the same as mother's wisdom. In a way that made me feel a little better, but all the anger just gave way to absolute helplessness. Finally I got up to leave.

"Goodnight," I said.

"Goodnight," he answered. I looked at his face, but his eyes were still on the floor.

"Thank you," I sniffed.

As he closed the door, I heard him whisper, "I'm sorry."

The next day was the worst of my life, the very worst. We were all awake at the crack of dawn. My husband had been up all night and although even the nurse pressed him to rest for the sake of his health, he continued in his jovial mood, saying he'd never made himself ill from staying up all night in the past and he would be fine. He sent the nurse to wake our daughter because her groom had already arrived to claim her.

I'll never forget the moment I heard the nurse's cries echoing down the staircase. I stumbled up there in my haste. I was terrified because somehow I knew what had happened. My daughter's silent compliance of the night before was a dreadful sign and yet I chose not to act upon it. What could I have done anyway? She asked me to leave. She said she wanted to be alone. She didn't even want her beloved nurse.

When I entered that room it was as though the world had frozen. It was ice cold in there, even though it was a summer's morning. I asked what was the matter. I don't know why I asked because I already knew. And then I saw her. So still and beautiful and perfect. She was my only child, she was the embodiment of all my hopes and dreams. How could this be?

Our cries brought my husband to the room. The shock of it took all the wind from his sails. What was there to say? What was there to do? Before we knew it the vicar and the bridegroom were in the room with us, asking if the bride was ready. My husband had to tell him that death had come before him to claim her as his bride. Now we had only death as an heir. We were all crying and lamenting, each with our own private grief of mother, father, lover, but all united in our shared loss.

The vicar began to speak of how heaven was blessed with her now and how heaven meant eternal life. The thought of eternal life in heaven was of little comfort to me. She was my one poor child and I would never see her again. The vicar said that her death was punishment for our sins. Didn't he know the guilt we all already felt?

I felt a horrible guilt that would stay with me forever. I was guilty for giving my daughter into the care of another woman. It was what I had to do, but I felt guilty that I was not the mother I would have liked to have been to her. It was not my choice, but still I let it happen. It was easier for me that way. There was always a distance between us. Perhaps I had even shown more favour to her cousin. Yes, I felt closer to him than to her in many ways and to her this must have seemed like a betrayal. I felt guilt that I had gone along with my husband's plans, not seeking to know how she really felt. It wouldn't have changed what we had to do, but it would have changed our relationship. Instead I let her die without asking her how she really felt. I accepted her happiness because it was convenient for me, but I ignored her misery when it got in the way of our plans for her. I let her down. I could have pressed my husband to wait longer, but I hadn't. I let her down and I felt guilty. I felt completely alone because my husband's grief was different from mine. We both had to suffer alone.

I could not understand what had happened. Just two days before she had been flushed with the excitement of new love. The change that came over her yesterday was hard enough to bear, but now this! The confusion *that I felt just compounded my guilt. I didn't really know her at all. I'd had no idea what was going on in her mind. She shared nothing with me of her private thoughts. We were like strangers, intimate strangers.*

Thirteen

The most bizarre turn of events was to follow. The poor young man who was supposed to be my girlie's bridegroom was beside himself with grief, as were all of us. He barely knew her, but he had set his heart on being her husband with an earnestness and devotion the likes of which I've rarely seen. He couldn't understand, no more than anyone else, what had happened. How could this beautiful angel be offered to him one day and then so cruelly taken from him the next? These extremes of joy and sorrow were hard for him to bear and he just couldn't make any sense of it. It seemed that she had died of the grief of losing her cousin. That's what *he* thought anyway. She had been so sensitive and he saw the depth of what he had lost. How much more it would have pained him to think that she had died rather than become his wife. He wasn't ashamed to show his tears and it made him no less manly in my eyes. His loss was great and it comforted me to know that others shared my own grief. I wanted to take him in my arms and stroke his hair like a mother. He went the next day to lay flowers around the chapel where she lay and he swore he would do that every day thereafter.

After two days, when the horrible reality was beginning to set in, a peculiar chain of events began to unfold. It was around dawn and there was all sorts of commotion going on. The night watchmen had been called and everyone was hurrying down to the chapel. There was blood on the steps and when they entered there was no trace of my girlie where she had lain. Instead, there was her fiancé, lying in her place, quite dead and covered in blood. What weird magic was this and what could explain it? The young man's valet was not far away. It was he who had called the watchmen. He had called for help in terror for his master's life and run off to find someone. It seems that his master had come to lay flowers in the chapel and while he was there he had been surprised by, of all people, that boy. What a shock to find him there at the family chapel of the young man he had killed. Of course the last thing he was going to think was that he had come because of my girlie. They began to quarrel and then to fight. That boy was wild and reckless and he acted in what seemed like a vengeful rage. The servant ran off to raise the alarm, but before he could return, his master lay dead and the perpetrator was nowhere to be found. And where was my girlie's body? What had he done with her? His father was sent for to witness what he had done and there we were, all assembled: the master and the mistress, that boy's father, the watchmen, the servants. We all took in the shocking scene.

But there *was* someone who could explain this bizarre mystery. It was the vicar. He was there too. He knew everything and as he told his tale the light began to dawn, both on the horizon and in our foggy minds. He didn't seem at all sure of himself, not like he had seemed just a few days ago. He was jittery and stuttered his way through his words. I think he was ashamed of what he had done and how it had turned out for the poor dead young man in my girlie's place. He kept looking at the floor. He couldn't meet anyone's eyes but mine, which was strange after how he had been when I went to see him the other night. Perhaps he hoped that I would somehow approve of what he had done because I had been involved too. He explained how he had married my girlie and that boy, the same day that he had killed her cousin. He looked to me to confirm it and I nodded, looking down for shame of my part in it. But then when he had to go away and my girlie was promised to another, she ran to the vicar, desperate for a solution to this impossible situation. That was when she had given up on me because I didn't say what she wanted to hear. She was frantic and threatened to kill herself if he didn't find a way to prevent this second marriage. This is what he had already told me, but he had only told me half of what had been said. His solution was a bold one. He gave her a sleeping potion which would simulate death. There was no pulse, or so it seemed. You couldn't tell that she was breathing. She would sleep for forty-two hours. In the meantime the vicar's plan was to send a message to her husband to tell him about the plan, so he could be there when she awoke and they could run away together. The vicar knew that he had gone into hiding in some remote part of the New Forest. On hearing this, a smile spread across my lips. What joy! My girlie was alive. What an incredible seesawing of emotions I was experiencing. One minute I was in despair and now my heart was singing within me. Who cared if I never saw her again? She was alive and she was happy with her husband.

The vicar went on. Things hadn't gone quite to plan. The problems started when they had one less day to make the arrangements. The master being so glad that his daughter had seen sense, had brought the whole thing forward by twenty-four hours. This made it hard to get the message to the boy in time. He tried to send another man of the church, but he wasn't able to get the message to him. By the time the man got back there were only a few hours left until my girlie would awake. In the meantime a servant lad from the boy's household had found him first and had given him the news that his new wife was dead. The bewildered lad, who was with the vicar now, explained how he had found his young master and given him the sad news of what was going on at home. He said he hardly knew how to tell him, he was so excited to hear news of his lady love. When he told him, the news made him desperate. The lad said he looked all pale and wild and it frightened him. He kept asking if there was a letter from the vicar for him. It seems that the next thing he did was to meet with some seedy drug dealer before rushing back home with wild thoughts in his mind. He had some poison. Would he have used it if he really had found his wife dead? One thing was for sure—he had come across the fiancé first. What senseless rage must have overtaken him. I said he was no good and there'd be no future pardon for him now. He had acted in cold blood, cold and vengeful blood. If he had intended to kill himself too and die beside his wife, then I don't see that as any sort of mitigating circumstance. As far as I was concerned he couldn't redeem himself by dying like a tragic hero. Tragic, maybe, but that wouldn't have been heroic, just stupid. And he wouldn't have been doing it for her, just for himself because he couldn't face his shame. There's no excuse for him. He didn't have to take another man with him. What could she possibly see in him? I still didn't understand it. Now she had thrown her life away all for this good-looking flatterer. He possessed her totally and to her he could do no wrong. Well, at least she was alive and well and I thanked the Lord for that.

As I was saying, the vicar told us how when his messenger returned without delivering his letter, he feared that something terrible was about to happen. What if that boy had heard what had supposedly happened to his beautiful wife? What if he came back with some desperate plan on his mind? The vicar knew he had to be there before my girlie awoke. He had to be there in case her husband came back and thought she was truly dead. So he rushed over to the chapel, but found that in some ways he was already too late. The commotion had started, my girlie's intended was lying dead and that boy was sobbing over his apparently lifeless wife. Nevertheless, the vicar said he was overwhelmed with relief that he was in time to stop any more craziness. He explained how he had taken hold of the boy by the shoulders and shaken him in a frenzy to make him come back to the here and now and understand what was happening. He said the boy was wailing and his breath was coming in huge sobbing heaves. The sound of his own breathing was so loud he seemed not to be able to hear what was being said to him.

"Look at me," said the vicar, grabbing him and pulling his shoulders round to face him which took all his strength. He said he feared for his own safety, the boy was so wild. The boy just kept screaming, "No, no, no. She's mine. This can't be." The vicar said he kept on saying, "It's not how it seems, it's not how it seems. Feel her, she's warm. This isn't death. Feel her." The boy held her up to his face. He kissed her still lips and held her close, rocking back and forth. His warm tears fell on her face. He suddenly stopped and looked at the vicar.

"What kind of trick is this?" he asked. "What have you done?" He kissed her again and felt the warmth. Was it the warmth of her life or of his own tears on her lips? He moved back to look at her with a look of incredulous confusion on his face. "What have you done?" he repeated, looking quizzically at the vicar. "Is she really alive? Is this a trick? What have you done?" As the vicar began to explain haltingly about the sleeping potion the boy looked down at my girlie. Her eyelids began to flicker and her lips to part. The vicar said that he bent to kiss her again, as though he was breathing new life into her. Her brow wrinkled and she opened her eyes and looked straight into the eyes of her husband. The vicar told us that he had never before witnessed such a moment of pure joy. My girlie was gasping with elation. It was just as the vicar had told her it would be—she awoke in the arms of her lover. The boy held her to him and squeezed her so tight, swaying from side to side in pure joy, his tears flowing again.

"Come on, come on," the vicar urged. "There's no time to waste. The alarm has been raised. You need to get away. You mustn't be found here." He said he virtually had to push them out into the breaking dawn to run off in the opposite direction from the village. Nothing was said about the poor dead young man in the chapel. He didn't even know if my girlie was aware of what had happened. She was just whisked away.

She was whisked away and she was alive. She was safe and my soul was floating. The sorrow of her loss was swept away and I was left with the simple joy of knowing that she was alive. Nothing else mattered to me. She left me without a goodbye, without sharing her plans with me. Oh, how easily I could forgive her that. My only sorrow was in my ignorance of whether *she* could ever forgive *me*. I stole glances at the vicar, but following his lead I kept my eyes on the ground for most of the time. I knew that I no longer had a job. My girlie was gone and there was nothing left for me to do in the household. The master and the mistress wouldn't have kept me there anyway after what I had known and what I had helped my girlie to do. They weren't going to have to ask me to leave. I'd pack up my stuff and slip away from their lives without a word.

What happened next made me glad to be gone from that house. When the vicar had finished his tale the air was tingling with all kinds of feelings. More than anything there was the shock. It was all so much to take in in such a short time. And there was tension. The vicar was tense with anxiety for how he would be punished for what he had done. There was the tension of the lingering hatred between the two families. There was the shock of this new death and the wretchedness of the poor man's unreturned love. There was the disbelief at the wilfulness and the audacity of the two young lovers. And floating above it all was my quiet joy. She wasn't gone from the world, just gone from me. I suppose that's the way of things. Just like a little bird in a nest. It starts out totally dependent and gradually gets ready to fly away, free and independent, never to return. All these feelings hung there in the stillness. Then the master broke the silence:

"Today we mourn," he said. "We mourn the loss of our children. For she is as dead to me now as when she lay there, still in this chapel." He spat the words out with venom. "I have wept for her loss and that is the end of her life." My eyes, still on the floor, widened in amazement. Could he really not be overjoyed that she was after all alive?

That boy's father then strode up to him and came so close, they would have felt each other's breath. "She stole my son's soul," he seethed. "She brought him to murder, to deceit and to shame. He defied all the principles of my family in making such a union. My son is gone. He might just as well have taken the poison. It would have been more honourable after what he has done. To me he is dead and I shall hold you responsible forever." His tone was low and deliberate. His eyes were narrow with hatred. The master thrust his chest forward like a strutting cockerel.

"I cannot let it be known that my daughter ran away with a murderer."

"And I, sir, cannot let it be known that my son was weak enough to be lured into such a trap, then ran from the scene like a coward. It is too shameful."

There was a long pause, a long and weighty pause.

"No one need ever know these things," declared the master finally. I was filled with the horror of it as I listened. "Those of you who came here this morning found a sorry scene indeed. You found these two lovers here dead. The boy came here with poison to end it all beside his beloved. She awoke and found him dead. Unable to bear life to continue without him she stabbed herself. You saw the blood." We were all silent. His voice was so cold. "We shall make it known that the two families are reconciled by our common tragedy. That we have shaken hands and wept together. In time this will all be forgotten. We shall not have to live with shame."

The boy's father glared at his enemy. "I'll agree to that," he said. "Our children have died tragically. Our lives will go on without them." I looked at his angry eyes. It seemed as though what bothered him most was the fact that my master had thought of this first.

"Yes," the vicar spoke up. I glared at him with disdain. "Yes," he repeated. "That is for the best. Today is a day of mourning. May God have mercy on their souls."

As everyone crossed themselves I turned my back and walked away from their hypocrisy. Mourning, my arse. God forbid anyone should know the awful embarrassing truth: that these two young people should have defied their families to love each other. Humph! I can live with that truth. He may have been a weaselly little toe rag, a hot-headed louse who was ruled by the emotions of the moment, but she loved him and I was glad that they were gone from here forever. I was only embarrassed by the pathetic attitude of these so-called ladies and gentlemen. I walked away from them. I went back to the house and packed up my few possessions and left. I never spoke to the master and the mistress again. I know they didn't want to speak to me and I was buggered if I had a decent word to say to them. What had they lost by her leaving them? I suppose they had lost their little prize to give away, their bargaining piece in the marriage game. She was supposed to bring them position and prestige and wealth. They preferred for her to be dead than to bring them shame and humiliation and embarrassment. And where was the shame in following your heart? Where was the humiliation in enjoying the thrill of loving and being loved? What cause was there for embarrassment when a child grows up to follow her own path? What did they understand about loving a child? It wasn't that they disapproved of him morally. It wouldn't have mattered to them if he had killed a member of his *own* family. It was just that he was who he was. What's in a name? To them *everything* was in the name. Actually it was convenient for the other family to have him believed dead. Then the whole affair would be over and done with for them and they could just get on with the everyday business of hating my girlie's family. Yes, death was much less embarrassing for all of them.

What an incredible turn of events. Now what had seemed so inexplicable to me, all suddenly made sense. There was an almighty commotion at dawn the next day. I could hear people calling out. I heard my daughter's name and her bridegroom's. People were also talking about that dreadful boy who had killed my nephew. Everyone was rushing to our family chapel and we were completely stunned to arrive there and find my daughter's poor groom lying dead in her place. What could the explanation be?

It was the vicar who shared with us the shocking truth. It was hardly believable. How could my daughter have been so taken in by that boy? How could she have participated in such a monstrous plan? How could she have defied us in this way and left us to grieve? How long had this all been going on? When I had first spoken to her of marriage it seemed like the idea had hardly ever crossed her mind. How long had she secretly loved the son of our enemy? How dare she scheme and plan in this manner when we were doing so much for her! The monstrousness of her ingratitude filled me with anger. I felt angry too that I had wasted my grief on her. I felt so taken advantage of. And I was the one who had been feeling guilty? She had betrayed my trust, my feelings and all that I had hoped for on her behalf.

As the vicar told his story I glanced at the nurse. She was smiling! So she knew all about it. She had known my daughter inside out and she had encouraged her in her deceitful behaviour. The whole thing was unforgivable. How could she presume to know what's best for my daughter? She had no right. She was just a servant and she had completely taken my place in my daughter's life. I felt so violated. What made her think that she knew better than I? And she had allowed her to throw her entire life away for nothing, for a wild infatuation. How irresponsible! And she was the adult. I never wanted to see her again.

That boy's conduct was completely unpardonable and not only had he got clean away with murder, but he had to steal my daughter from me too! It wasn't enough for him to take one young life from us. It was atrocious. It was outrageous. And to kill that poor, earnest young man as well. How could such a monster have bewitched my daughter in such a manner? I just shuddered at the thought of it. She would no longer be my daughter.

My husband's proposal, that we should mourn them as if they truly had died was the perfect solution. They were dead to us. The daughter that I was mourning was indeed dead to me. They were gone and they would never return. They might as well be dead. We would have the same loss from which to recover. We would grieve and we would mourn and we would go on with our life. This was preferable to the shame of what had really happened. I cared not one jot whether we should give the appearance of having healed the rift between the two families, but my husband insisted upon it and his enemy agreed, albeit reluctantly. There was my husband again, always the magnanimous one. I could always love him. I had no child to love.

Fourteen

So that's how things were left. All was quiet for a while. Everyone acted exactly according to what had been said on that grey morning. Those who had been there kept their silence. They all thought it was better for everyone that way. The lovers were gone from their lives. Dead, alive, mourned, forgotten … what was the difference? The feud was suspended, at least temporarily, for appearances' sake. It looked better that way and anyway the worst of the young hotheads were dead (or "dead"). Tragedy was less embarrassing than disgrace. Loss was less awkward than dishonour.

My employers dealt with their loss by burying themselves in their business interests. It was truly a great loss to them no longer to have the one prize that could buy them wealth and influence for the future, so they concentrated on the power and prosperity they could command for the time being. They had the general sympathies of the powers that be for the magnitude of their loss and it made me quietly furious that they would use the tragedy that never was for financial and social gain. What a bunch of snobs who think it's more important to *look* right than to *do* right.

The other family were no better. They were happy to play along and keep things quiet. Above all they wanted to preserve the family name. The name was more important to them than the people. They just had to write that boy off and get on with keeping up appearances. The pretence that the feud was over made it a little easier for them. It made them all look better. How *wonderful* that they could put aside all that animosity to be united in grief. Grief, my arse. They were united in hypocrisy. They had come together for the sake of an enormous lie. It was indeed much better for the family name for him to be thought of as a tragic hero than as the low down murderous bastard that he really was. So everyone was happy. *His* family too, turned their attentions to the more important matter of making money.

Even the servants cooled off their constant name-calling and street-fighting for a while. They just did as they were told. They only ever did what they were told after all—if they wanted to remain in gainful employment. I was glad to be out of there because I couldn't have handled it. I loved my girlie. I couldn't pretend my feelings about her and I was glad that she was out of it too. Yes, I had lost her, but I kept on telling myself that it was the good sort of loss that a mother experiences when her child goes away to make her own life. It was that bitter joy. Of course I missed her and I missed her just as I would have done if she really *had* been dead. Every day there was some little thing that I wanted to tell her, just like with my poor husband, God rest his soul. It *was* a kind of mourning because I missed her so much, but it was mixed with that incredible joy I had felt when I had realised that she was still alive. And that was enough for me. I went back to my old life. The life I had before she was even born. I took in some sewing work, just to keep me from going hungry and I had enough to keep me busy. It kept me from missing her too much to have something to do. It was good to be ignored by the people I used to work for. After all, if they hadn't been so busy acting like I didn't exist, I would have had the pleasure of giving *them* the cold shoulder. No matter. They could get on with their hypocrisy as far as I was concerned. It was no skin off *my* nose and I was better off going back to my good old honest life, than having anything to do with the likes of them. There would be enough sewing work for me to do even without embroidering their fancy tablecloths.

And what of that poor young man who had so wanted to make my girlie his bride? They put out the story that he had been attacked and left to die by robbers and his demise was all but forgotten as having had anything to do with the two young lovers who had died for the sake of their forbidden love. Nothing was ever said about where his body was found and his family were happier not to ask too many questions. They were only too happy to be distanced from the whole sordid affair. In a way he *was* attacked by a robber—that boy had robbed him of his beautiful bride and then robbed him of his life. Again, it was the path of least embarrassment to accept one kind of crime over another.

The vicar left. He couldn't be a part of the lie and he had lost the confidence of the powerful families because of his part in conspiring against them to allow the lovers to be together. He was lucky that they didn't want the truth to be known. It was convenient for all of them for him to go away and minister to the souls in some other community. The bishop was kept in the dark as to the truth of the matter. He was a blithering old fart anyway and he couldn't see any farther than the end of his wrinkled old nose. I did see the vicar one more time before he left. I bumped into him on the road. He was carrying basketsful of I don't know what, getting ready to pack up and leave.

"I see you're getting on with your life," I said. "No point in sitting around grieving."

"Er ... no," he muttered, glancing at me quickly, then dropping his gaze to the ground.

"Well that's nothing to be ashamed of," I went on. "No use crying over spilt milk. That's what I always say. After all, life goes on, eh?" I grinned at him and he stole another quick glance at me, trying to decide if I was on the level or if I was just taking the piss. I smiled a cheesy smile and he blushed the colour of a raspberry. Served him right if you ask me.

"We did the right thing," he faltered.

"Speak for yourself," I countered, all prim and proper.

"Things are better this way," he said. "They are gone and they are together."

"And those of us that are left behind have only our consciences to deal with."

"Yes," he said haltingly, "yes, quite so." This was barely a whisper.

"Humph!" I snorted in contempt. "Well good luck to you. Go off and make a new start. It seems to be the thing to do."

"Yes," he said slowly. "Quite so." And he started to move off in the way he had been going.

"God bless you," he almost whispered as he walked away.

I don't suppose he heard me muttering, "God, my arse," as I turned around and strode away from him.

The aftermath of the whole affair was not pleasant. We observed a period of mourning and made sure that it was generally known that the two families had made peace in their mutual sorrow. It was in fact a peaceful time. It was a relief at least not to have to think about that unpleasant aspect of our life for a while. I was tired of it and the loss of the children, especially my nephew, had brought home to me the pointlessness of it all. I hoped that the "truce" would persist for at least our period of mourning, if not forever.

Our enemies kept themselves to themselves during that time and mercifully our paths did not have to cross.

I was thankful then to have my wise and splendid husband. He conducted himself with such quiet dignity. I was proud to be his wife. He never mentioned our daughter. He did indeed mourn and I know that he missed her terribly. He missed her sunny disposition. He missed her beauty and her playfulness. He missed her presence in our home. He concentrated on business, to keep himself from thinking of her, but I know that this didn't really work for him. I never mentioned her to him either. The pain was too great for him.

The nurse disappeared from our lives. We never spoke to her after that morning at the chapel. She at least had the sense to pack her bags and be gone before we had to throw her out. I was left to think about that smile I had seen on her face that morning. It was almost a smirk. She thought that she had won some sort of victory over us. Well she was the one left without a way to make her living. She was the one who had to slink away like a criminal. It served her right. Did she think that that was the way to show the girl she cared about her? To let her have her way? Not to intervene to make her see sense and to save her from such a horrible fate? The secret lovers were no doubt laughing at her gullibility for having helped them. I felt as though the woman had stolen something from me. I should have been the one the girl turned to for advice. I wouldn't have let her get into this terrible mess. I would have made her see sense. Now the nurse was left with nothing. At least I had my husband and we still had our place in the world.

The vicar was rightly ashamed of himself. The sooner he was away from us the better. He could no longer hope to command the respect of any decent people in this parish. He was transferred to somewhere far away. I only hope he had learned his lesson and would not jeopardize the lives of any of the members of his future congregation. I didn't want to hear any more about him. I'm glad I don't know where he went. I don't even want to think about him. How could he call himself a man of God, while participating in such sins? He has helped the boy on his way to hell!

And how did I manage in those days following our terrible loss? How would any mother manage? The loss of a child is unimaginable. And I had lost her. One way or another she was gone from me forever. They would never come back. Even if they did, I would never acknowledge her. She was dead and death is forever. There would be no resurrection. I would wonder from time to time what she thought of me. Did she ever think of me? If she did was it with disdain, was it with regret? I would never know. I liked to think that there would be something of regret. I yearned to share these thoughts with my husband, but I could not. I was condemned to keep them hidden inside me and pray that over time they would recede into the background of my life and I would think of her less and less.

Fifteen

And then she came home to me. She had burnt all her other bridges, but not mine. She must always have known that. She knew she could always come home to me. I was still her island of comfort. That invisible cord had stretched and stretched, but it had never broken and now she had come back home to me. I wasn't expecting her, not then, but then I wasn't surprised either. It wasn't hard for her to find me. All she had to do was go to the village pub and ask. Thank goodness I stayed in the village. It wasn't that long since I had seen her, six months maybe. It was winter and the air was heavy like a cold, wet blanket. Once she was gone I had hoped she would be gone for good, that I had been wrong about him, about that kind of man. But he was still a boy. I had hoped that love had made a man of him. Perhaps he would understand the real stuff love was about: about living with someone for always and accepting the way they are, not wanting them to be the love you have dreamed up in your head. He should have accepted what she had given up for him and seen the value of the gift she gave him when she gave him her whole self.

With one look I could see that he had made a woman of her. She had come to me because there was nowhere else to go with her bulging belly. She looked down, feeling shame, but I picked up her chin and looked into those blue eyes. My own eyes told her the whole story of love that lasts for ever.

"My girlie," I said softly and my arms enveloped her as she gave in to waves of grief. She grieved for all that she had lost. She grieved for her lost love, for her lost home, her lost pride.

"I'm sorry," came through her sobs. She was wet: wet with winter raindrops and her own tears.

"Now what would you have to be sorry about?" I whispered. Her breath came in jerky rasps as she tried to get the words out through her tears. "I should have listened to you."

"It's all right," I whispered.

"You said it was time to do what they wanted." She managed a deep breath and the tears flowed. "I should have listened to you."

"Shhhh." I held her close like I always had.

"I'm sorry, I should have listened."

"Sometimes you have to find your own way," I said. She wiped her dripping nose with the back of her hand. I wiped her cheek, gently, with love.

"I cut you out," she wailed, "and you were right."

"None of that matters now," I heard myself saying and it was true. "All that matters is that you are home with me and I'll take care of you."

I shut out the cold of the January night and led her to the fireside where she slumped down in the waiting chair.

Her story was a long one. They had fled in haste, hardly stopping for breath. They were many miles away before they even talked about what had happened. Well, they had never really talked about anything. The whole affair had taken place in just a few days. They were married before they had ever even had a real conversation. They were just breathless and intoxicated in their state of adolescent love.

"I loved him," she said simply. "I just loved him. There didn't seem to be any need for words. I would have done anything, gone anywhere for him. I did. I left my home, I left my family, I left you. I must have been crazy with it. I let you think I was dead. How could I have been so cruel to you? How will you ever be able to forgive me?" And she broke down in sobs again.

I shushed her again and rocked her in my arms, on my knees by her chair. "That's the whole point," I said. "There's no question of it. The kind of love I feel for you goes way beyond all that. I am here for you and that is the way it will be forever. It doesn't change because of something you do or say. Yes, I can be hurt, but I can always forgive. Anyway, I didn't stop you. Can *you* forgive *me?*"

"No, you didn't stop me, but you *would* have if I had only listened." This was true and she shuddered with a new round of sobs.

"That's because I didn't love him and you did. It was already too late for me to stop you. You were too far gone." She sniffed in acknowledgement.

"It was so exciting," she said "to run away with him, to forget all about the rest of the world and just be completely wrapped up in our love. I really would have gone anywhere. He was so wonderful. I couldn't think. I just acted. When you have that all-encompassing love it keeps you safe. You don't need anyone else. The rest of the world can just melt away and you wouldn't even notice. But when that's gone, you look around and you realise you're all alone." She raised her swollen eyes to me. "That's when you realise how important the rest of the world is and you feel so ashamed. *I* felt ashamed. I acted like you didn't exist, as if I didn't need you, but I was wrong. I'm so ashamed that I didn't think about you."

"That's the way things are," I answered her simply. "When the baby birds have grown, they fly the nest. It means the parents have struggled and worried and they've done their job. The young are ready to make their own lives. When you left I was happy. I was overjoyed that you were still alive to make your own life. That was enough for me: just the fact that you were alive." The tears were coming for me too now. "When they were all standing around in the chapel there and the vicar was telling his story, explaining it all ... At that moment, when I realised what had happened, when I realised that you weren't dead after all, I wanted to scream out and hug everyone. Yes, it was a bitter joy because I thought I'd never see you again, but it must have been just about the biggest joy of my life." I looked at her and I smiled and she smiled back, the biggest beaming smile I'd seen in I don't know how long. We understood each other. We hugged again and now we were both weeping tears of joy. Had she doubted how I would greet her?

Had she thought that she really was alone in the world? If she had, the doubts were all swept away now. She had learnt a lesson about love, the kind of love that doesn't change. You don't have to be a fine lady to know this love. Just a woman. Just a mother.

I waited, just enjoying the feeling. When she was ready she would tell me more. First there were the tears and the smiles. She was even able to laugh her sunny laugh for me. What a fine mess that boy had brought her to, but what a joy it was for me to be her refuge. We were both quiet for a while.

"When he told me about what had happened to my fiancé, I was so shocked. I was even frightened. He said that he was coming to die beside me. He wanted to be a romantic hero. Was that heroic? He said that when he came across the poor man, he was crying over me, laying flowers in my memory. I didn't know that he even cared. I had never given him a thought other than as part of my father's plan to give me away to the highest bidder. He found my husband with a crowbar, trying to get into the chapel and he challenged him. He knew nothing of our relationship and thought that he must have come to desecrate the bodies or something. My poor dead cousin was in there with me, you see. He was only trying to defend me, even when he thought I was already dead. I grieved when I heard of his fate and that made my husband angry. It was the first harsh words he had spoken to me and I was even more shocked. Where did all this anger come from? He said he had done all this for me and I should be happy. There was a wild look in his eyes that I hadn't seen before and it frightened me." She covered her face with her hands. She told me how she had tried not to think about it. There was no going back now. Instead she concentrated on their love and put everything else out of her mind.

"Once that had happened, things were never quite the same. He had shown me another side of himself and although it didn't change my love for him, it was always there, under the surface and I was frightened to say any more about it. He seemed to think that I should be completely loyal to him in all things and if I said that what he had done had shocked me or scared me, then I was being disloyal. So I just kept it inside me, but that meant that there was the beginning of a barrier between us." Well this was no shock to me and I told her so. If only they had had the time to allow a real relationship to develop, before all this rashness and mayhem set in.

She went on with her story: "I don't know when he began to change, but he did."

"Perhaps he didn't change at all," I murmured. "Perhaps he just showed you different sides of himself. You just got to know him better and better." She didn't challenge me on this. I know I was right. I suppose she knew it too, but it was too painful for her to think about.

"We didn't have a plan and we didn't have much to live on, just a few things we could sell. We were living in inns and bed and breakfasts, moving on when it became obvious that we couldn't pay our bills. When I realised I was pregnant I told him we needed to have a plan. He needed to work so we could live. This made him angry. He said it was all my fault. It was because of me he had thrown everything away and now he had no future. This hurt me so much after everything I had given up to be with him. He said horrible cruel things about my family, about my cousin he had killed. He said he had no choice and it was all because of me. And how could he say we had no future when we had this baby on the way that we had created out of our love?" She covered her face with her hands and began sobbing quietly. My heart ached for her, for the disappointment she had suffered. It would have given me no pleasure to say to her, "Told you so." I put my hands on her shoulders and felt her shuddering with her misery.

"My girlie," I said. She leaned her head against my breast like she did when she was a little girl and gave in again to her tears.

"My girlie," I repeated in a whisper and I rocked her like a baby. "I'm here, I'm here."

As she sat there by the fire, she gradually got warm and as she told her story she seemed to feel gradually better, as though her misery was evaporating along with the cold dampness. No, that boy didn't change.

She just came to see him in a different way. As he began to feel burdened by her and her condition, he made less and less effort to speak to her of love. Well, there was no point now. The excitement was over. He had won her and he was stuck with her. There was certainly no going back for him. He began to understand that the thrill of the chase and the knowledge of possession were two very different things. He could no longer moon around like a love-sick cow. All his poetry and wooing had won him a prize he didn't want to take responsibility for. Now he felt trapped by it and he told her so, cruelly and often. If this was growing up, it wasn't what he'd meant to do at all. This certainly wasn't the love he had dreamed of.

She said that he began to spend less and less time with her. As they moved from inn to inn he found new places he could go to drink and be away from her. Eventually there were nights when he didn't come home to her. He was out all night, just to be away from her and his responsibility. She imagined him with other women, but dared not challenge him on it because she feared his anger. He told her she was weighing him down as she became rounder, carrying the burden of their love. What did he want this for? Oh what a mess! My poor girlie. She was too young to be learning this kind of lesson about love and life. The third or fourth time when he had stayed out all night and she had said nothing, he wouldn't keep the silence that was keeping her safe from his cruelty.

"Don't you want to know where I have been?" he railed. "Don't you want to know who I was with?"

"No," she whispered. She didn't want to know. It was painful enough for her to think it. She didn't want to hear it from him. But he didn't care about what she wanted or didn't want.

"I was with a girl," he said and his words cut through her like a knife. "A beautiful girl. One who wants to give me love. One who has not ruined my life." And he turned away from her. She sobbed silently, feeling all wrung out and empty. Where could she find comfort in her desperation if not from him? Thank heavens she knew the answer to that!

She silently made her decision. It wasn't really a sudden decision. I suppose she had known from the minute she ran away with him; from the minute she really realized what he had done. What a bastard. She made her decision. The next time he left her alone, he would not find her there when he came back. If she and her baby had become a burden to him, then he would be free of them. She needed to be sheltered by love and his love had shrivelled like grapes left on a vine to rot.

And now she looked at me, her eyes open wide in innocence; the innocence of the child she still was, despite the woman's body she displayed for all the world to see. "I remembered," she said quietly and I listened, knowing what she was going to say, but still waiting for her to say it, as if the saying of it somehow gave it more weight, more truth. "I remembered what you always used to say. I remembered that your love is always with me." She smiled shyly. I suppose that now, with everything that had happened, this didn't seem quite so silly to her. It was a joy to me that now she knew it, that I wasn't just a daft old bat saying empty things to rattle around in her mind for a moment and then be gone. I always meant it and now she understood. It had given her the courage to leave him and the determination to come home to me. It had kept her going through this soggy, miserable winter to get home. Home is where the heart is they say. If you can build a new home with love, then that's where you should be, but if the foundations are too rocky then it will all come crashing down and the only safe place is the home you came from, the love you came from. Home is where the people you love are. I suppose I too needed a home. Since she'd been gone I had been alone. I was alone for the first time in my life. It is strange to be alone and know that your love is somewhere else. At least I had that. At least I knew she was somewhere, the girlie I loved. I knew she was out there somewhere in that big world, loving me back in a quiet way, while she got on with her life.

I rocked her as she smiled through her tears and we spent a long silent moment together, understanding, remembering the bond we always had, warm and safe in mother's love. She was exhausted, but she was full of relief that she no longer had to bear her burden alone, that there were no secrets, that there was nothing that could take this feeling of safety away from her. I made her a warm drink and insisted that she ate something, though she said she wasn't hungry. It was my pleasure to do my job of mothering her. It was the best thing I had ever done and now she needed me in a whole new way. As we sat together by the fire I felt a closeness with her that I could never have imagined I had the right to hope for again. Children don't owe their parents anything. It's the other way round. They have to live with the mistakes we make and learn to make sense of the world from what we share with them. They are our joy; we owe it to them to make their lives the best they can be. That night when she gave in to her fatigue and I lay with her on my bed to get her off, I thought of all those times I did that when she was a child. And when she was asleep I stroked her hair and kissed her forehead. I always loved to kiss her when she was sleeping. It was my silent way of knowing that all was well at the end of the day. It was my way of saying I love you. My love is always with you, even when you're sleeping. On this night I whispered it to her, like I had done so many times before. She was safe. She was home.

I heard a rumour the following winter that my daughter had returned. No one returns from the dead. I let it be known in the household that this was just an idle rumour. No one returns from the dead indeed. But the rumour was more detailed than that: she had returned pregnant, carrying the child of the murderer. How abominable that thought was to me. It was somehow harder to bear than not knowing what had happened to her. I have heard that the mothers of missing children say that the worst part is not knowing what has happened to their loved ones, but to me this makes no sense. I preferred to think of her as out there "somewhere", perhaps in heaven, perhaps just living an ordinary life, perhaps happy, perhaps sad.

My fantasy would be as good as the reality. It turned out that it was better than the reality. While I didn't know, I could be the mistress of her destiny. It could all turn out exactly the way I dictated. But knowing the truth brought back all the sordidness of the whole affair.

Still I could not speak about it to my husband. He raised the subject once, I think just to make it clear to me that he would not speak of her as being alive.

"I have heard strange rumours about our dead daughter," he said.

I looked at him, wondering what to say. I knew he was suffering. Did he want to speak of her or just let me know that he would not?

"I am amazed what people will imagine for the sake of gossip," he went on. "Don't they know how hurtful it is to invent such things?"

I knew only too well how hurtful it could be to say such things of my beautiful lost daughter.

"No one returns from the dead," I said.

"Exactly," was his barely audible reply. "No one."

This was the only time we ever spoke of her. I stood next to him at his desk and put my hand on his. He looked up at me from his chair and I saw the tears again. I was overwhelmed with love for him. There was nothing I could do to ease his suffering, except be there with him. I couldn't speak of it. That would have made it harder for him. I just had to be there for him, silently observing his tears. They were not unmanly. They were human.

There was gossip though and I strained my ears to hear it. It was said that my daughter had found her way back to the nurse who had welcomed her with open arms. How was it that after all that she had done, that woman was rewarded, while I continued to be punished? This went against everything I knew about justice. She had offended against her employers. She was guilty of deceit and betrayal, yet she was compensated. I was a victim and yet for some reason I was condemned to a life sentence of misery and heartache. Where is the justice in that, I ask you? Where is the justice?

Sixteen

Over the next few months I helped her build her nest. We talked often of the future, of the life we would build together and how this baby would bring her the joy that I know so well. We never talked of him, although I know she thought of him often. I think that somehow she wanted to remember the good times and to think of this baby as the creation out of the good and pure love she had felt. I knew when she was thinking of him. She would look out beyond where her eyes could focus and they would fill with silent tears. What sweet sorrow she knew in recalling the beginning. She would lay her hands on her belly and smile at me through her tears. This baby was going to be her joy, her compensation.

I told her so many stories about when she was a baby. I told her about the day of her birth. I told her about my birth experience, even though she was born to another woman. Somehow I still needed to talk about it and sharing it with her helped me to heal some of those hurts that had been hidden away for all those years. It gave us something intimate to share, now that she was going to become a mother too. I told her how I laboured to bring my baby into the world. It was a long and hard labour. My poor husband, God rest his soul, was so helpless. He must have spent thirty-six hours just pacing and pacing, knowing this was women's stuff, yet wanting to help anyway. He was so anxious for me. He was scared that he might lose me. Yes, he was scared for the baby too, but he couldn't think about that. The baby wasn't really real to him yet. I remember the first time I asked him if he wanted to feel the baby kicking. He placed his hand so gently on my bulge and it was like magic to him when he felt it. But when I asked him another time if he wanted to feel it, he said no, he had done that already. I suppose he just wasn't involved with every intimate detail of that baby as I was. And then when I was in labour it was coming all too soon for him. It was such a big responsibility having created this new person and he would have to take care of both of us. I think that however the labour had gone, he would have been just as scared. He was scared to see me in pain and he was scared not knowing what was really normal. He felt responsible for giving me the pain too, I think, like it was all his fault. I think the midwife knew how it was going to turn out, but she kept encouraging me and telling what to do to get that baby out. It's amazing what reserves of strength you have when you really needed it. I pushed and pushed for hours and it seemed like I wasn't getting anywhere. The midwife was so business-like and calm, just telling me what to do. She pushed too, leaning against me to give me more strength.

And just when I thought I couldn't do it any more, she would make me look in her eyes and she'd say, "You can and you will." And I did. I don't know how I found those reserves of strength when I was so exhausted. But I did it. When the baby finally slithered out of me and I saw that she was purple and still, all I could think of at that moment was thank God that's out of me. But then the silence went on. There was no cry and there was an icy stillness in the room and that moment lasted forever. The midwife handed my warm, wet baby to me. All she said was, "I'm sorry." I clutched at that tiny bundle and my tears came. How could this have happened? How could I have gone through so much for this grief? And I felt a rush for guilt for having felt relieved that it was over. Telling all this to my girlie brought us close. I realized how much I needed to tell it and I felt better for the telling of it. She had always been my baby, my girlie, but somehow now I felt that sharing this with her finally made her truly my daughter.

She told me about her dreams. In one of them she was breastfeeding her baby and the baby was a girl and somehow, in the wonderful way of things that can only be possible in dreams, at the same time she *was* that baby and she could taste the warm, sweet milk. Was it a dream about the past or about the future or both? It has always amazed me that when you look into the face of a newborn baby you are looking at a whole person. She is a baby and a little girl, a new mother and an old lady, all at the same time. Everything is in there, like a tiny acorn is the seed of a great and ancient oak. Everything is contained in that seed: the past, the present, the future. Everything goes around like a big circle with no beginning and no end. Such is life.

We prepared together for the new spring. My girlie was blooming like the crocuses in the garden, fresh and new after the hard winter. By the time the baby would be born the tulips would be in bloom and the world would be full of warm sunshine and colour. I could hardly wait to support her, to be the one to protect her from the world, to mother the mother. We talked endlessly about how the labour might go and how I would be there holding her hand when she needed me. All was forgiven between us and we were like two conspiring schoolgirls. This was such a pleasure for me: to be able to be there for her at such a special time. What a fool that boy was, not to want to share this with her, but his loss was my gain. When she left I had been happy to forego this time with her. It was enough for me that she was alive and happy and this joy was for *him* to share. But now he had chosen his own path, now he had given up his role in my girlie's life and that of his baby, well now I could step in. I could be the one to hold her hand, to comfort her, to look forward with her and to protect her. I was full of a smugness that didn't quite say I told you so, but I felt like I had the right to it.

March turned to April and the daffodils bowed to the tulips. Now was the time. It began gradually, the slow ebb and flow of her contractions in the early hours of a Friday morning. She didn't even wake me. She wasn't sure if this was really it. As the day wore on she became more and more aware of what was happening inside her and she began to concentrate with all her strength on working with her body. She would close her eyes and picture in her mind her baby moving down to meet her, to come into her arms. Towards evening it got harder and I knew it was time to run for the midwife. I didn't want to leave her alone for a minute, but I knew that the longer I left it, the harder it would be to leave her. I really did run and it felt like forever that I was gone from her side. No woman in labour should be alone and when I raced back to her I held out my hands to get to her all the sooner. She grabbed them and squeezed so hard through her contraction that I was feeling it along with her. The midwife was so calm. That night I felt a complete solidarity with all the mothers of the world. This was not only the birth of a baby; it was the birth of a mother. My girlie was partaking of the secret of life just like I had done and I understood what she was feeling. We were part of the sisterhood of women everywhere. A little after midnight the bag of waters broke and the intensity of the contractions increased. It took all our will and our concentration to keep her centred and working with her body. What incredible strength a woman in labour can find within herself. The power of birth, the power of a mother's body is truly awesome. She must have pushed for two hours with all the strength she could muster. She leaned against me and I pushed with her. I helped her labour. It was another birth for me and my tears flowed for the joy and the sheer physical release.

With the greyness of the new dawn my girlie gave birth. She reached down and touched the soft, warm, wet head and she delivered her baby, slipping easily into her own hands. We heard the baby's cry only briefly. My girlie knew what to do. She brought her new baby girl to her breast and there she nuzzled in that all-encompassing security that only a mother's body can give. We cried. I looked deep into my girlie's eyes and saw them shining with new knowledge and with new love. We both cried and laughed and marvelled at this amazing new being.

The baby was a girl and she named her in honour of the one whose loss had brought us together. What a joy it was to see her alive and at her mother's breast. Neither of them noticed when the cord was cut. They were still together as a single unit, the one dependent on the other. The sun rose on that spring morning and we knew the pure joy of a new beginning. In the simple act of nursing her baby my girlie was making the world a better place. This is where giving and receiving meet. They are one and the same thing. Watching them I knew that this had been the most perfect thing in my own life. I smiled. I cried. I was healed. Life was good and now I was sure of it.

In the spring there were more rumblings and rumours. Her baby was born. It was a beautiful baby girl. I wondered if she would finally understand what I must be going through to have lost my daughter. She now knows what it is to be a mother, to have a daughter. But her situation is different. She will hold her baby and love her. No one will take her from her. She will watch her grow. She will be the first to see her smile. She will watch her first steps. She will comfort her when she falls down and she will dry her tears. She will laugh with her and cry with her and she will be the most important person in her life.

And she will have another woman supporting her, helping her through the hard times, but it won't be me. It should have been me. It should be me holding that baby and handing her back to her when she needs her mother. It should be me taking care of her when she is too exhausted to take care of herself. It should be me sleeping in the next room just in case she needs me. It should be my *privilege, but it is not.*

I am left with my regrets and my meagre memories. Does she ever think of me? Of her father who misses her so, but will not speak of her? Is she happy? Would it be too much to ask to have just one small share in that happiness? Would it be too much to ask, just to have the chance to say I'm sorry?

Epilogue

In the end there are some things that never change. A mother's love lasts forever. My girlie is coming to know this too. She will always have her precious child and she will always have me. The whole ghastly mess of her first love has left her with something she will always treasure. When a child grows up you can never ask her to choose between her mother and the man she loves. She would always choose him and that's the way it should be. That means you've done your job as a mother. At the same time it would never really be a choice anyway, because you will always be there waiting to give her the love and comfort you have always given her; just waiting in case she needs you. She can't go without your love. Not ever. Can I say that this is a happy ending? A mother's love lasts forever and there is nothing that can taint that. She will always have me. You see, I *am* her mother.

978-0-595-45871-4
0-595-45871-8

Made in the USA
Lexington, KY
10 December 2009